FINAL DOORS

By Joe L. Hensley

FINAL DOORS

JOE L. HENSLEY

PUBLISHED FOR THE CRIME CLUB BY
DOUBLEDAY & COMPANY, INC.
GARDEN CITY, NEW YORK
1981

Library of Congress Cataloging in Publication Data

Hensley, Joe L., 1926–
Final doors.

1. Detective and mystery stories, American. I. Title.
PS3558.E55F5   813'.54
AACR2
ISBN: 0-385-17800-X
Library of Congress Catalog Card Number 81-43254
Copyright © 1981 by Joe L. Hensley
All Rights Reserved
Printed in the United States of America
First Edition

Acknowledgments

"Trial Tactics," copyright 1980 by Davis Publications, Inc.
Reprinted from *Alfred Hitchcock's Mystery Magazine*.

"The Calculator," copyright 1979 by Davis Publications, Inc.
Reprinted from *Alfred Hitchcock's Mystery Magazine*.

"Widow," copyright 1980 by Laura W. Haywood and Isaac Asimov.
Reprinted from *Who Done It*, edited by Alice Laurence and Isaac Asimov.

"Pride in Performance," copyright 1981 by Eugene DeWeese and Joe L. Hensley.

"One Will Too Many," copyright 1966 by Leo Margulies Corp.
Reprinted from *The Man from U.N.C.L.E. Magazine*.

"The Chicken Player," copyright 1967 by Magnum-Royal Publications, Inc.
Reprinted from *Swank*.

"Lord Randy, My Son," appeared originally in *Dangerous Visions*, edited by Harlan Ellison; copyright © 1967 by Harlan Ellison. Copyright reassigned 1979. Copyright © 1979 by Joe L. Hensley.

"Do-It-Yourself" appeared originally in *Rogue* magazine; copyright © 1961 by Greenleaf Publishing Company. Copyright reassigned 1965. Copyright © 1965 by Harlan Ellison and Joe L. Hensley. All rights reserved.

"Argent Blood," copyright 1967 by Mercury Press, Inc.
Reprinted from *The Magazine of Fantasy and Science Fiction*.

"Rodney Parish for Hire" appeared originally in *Swank* magazine; copyright © 1962 by Royale Publications, Inc. Copyright reassigned by subsequent owners of the magazine title 1981. Copyright © 1981 by Harlan Ellison and Joe L. Hensley. All rights reserved.

This book is dedicated to Gene DeWeese, who collaborated on "Pride in Performance," and Harlan Ellison, who collaborated on "Do-It-Yourself" and "Rodney Parish for Hire." Good friends, boon companions.

CONTENTS

FINAL DOORS

TRIAL TACTICS

A month after I was admitted to the bar, my senior partner came to the door of my sparsely furnished office. Our shared quarters were on the second floor of a crumbling old building. But it was, at least, convenient to the courthouse.

"Busy?" he asked diffidently.

We weren't yet used to each other.

I waved the advance sheet I was reading. "Not really, Senator." I'd already learned that a good part of my time was going to be spent keeping up with the latest fancies of the appellate courts.

"We," ex-Senator Adams said, "are going to prosecute a murder case next week." He smiled, looking like a man who'd bitten into a lemon, but that was the only way he could smile.

My partner had served three terms in the state senate and so was called, for now and always, Senator Adams. He was a tall thin man who looked something like an Abe Lincoln gone to seed. People said he'd once been a lawyer of true distinction. He'd semiretired when he'd decided not to run again for the senate, but then his wife had become sick and the expenses of her long terminal illness had forced him back into practice.

He wore suits that were even more rumpled than mine. He was old and he looked perpetually tired, but I'd found him to be a scholarly man with a keen and wary brain. He'd spent much of the first month learning about me, asking me questions, giving me his answers. The first day in his office, for example, he'd asked me about ethics. I'd fumbled around for a time trying to recall all the dos and don'ts until he'd finally told me that for him being ethical was being able to face himself in the mirror each new day.

Back to the present. "I thought we *defended* criminal cases," I said.

"Normally that's true," he said. He shook his aging head and scuffed an embarrassed foot against the linoleum floor. "But my friend and yours, Coger Rock, the prosecuting attorney, has to go into the hospital tomorrow for surgery. Time's running out on the Briscoe Henzmann murder case, and Briscoe either gets prosecuted next Monday or he gets out. His attorney filed a motion for a speedy trial, and Monday's the last day. So Rock's named us—or me—as special prosecutor."

"Why you?" I asked.

"Several reasons. I've tried cases against the attorney defending the case. I also once represented the chief prosecuting witness, Briscoe's sister Edith, in an estate claim a few years back. Maybe—even probably—the murder grew out of that. And I know Briscoe. He's been in prison several times. Rock believes I don't like Briscoe. Come with me, Robak—let's go over to Coger's office." He lemonsmiled again and I observed he was wearing a badly frayed shirt again. "Helping me with the case will be good experience, and you'll even get paid for it."

I got to my feet, my day brightened by the unusual prospect of money.

Coger Rock sat fatly in his oversized chair. He was an obese man I much admired. I'd known him in law school where he'd been a year ahead of me. As a prosecutor I'd found him to be fair. He preferred no one.

"Senator Adams and Don Robak," he wheezed in greeting. "Sit down. Knowing you were due I took the liberty of asking Lieutenant Robbins, jack-of-all-trades for the Bington Police property room, to come up. I asked him to bring the principal item of evidence along for you to see."

Lieutenant Robbins was holding a tiny wrapped package. He carefully unwrapped it and placed it ostentatiously on Rock's desk. It was an aspirin bottle, partly filled with something.

"That's our baby," he said. "It doesn't look like much, but it might be enough to cook Briscoe Henzmann. We found it in his bedroom closet. I did a fingerprint test on it and lifted one of Briscoe's prints off it."

"Briscoe kept a supply of strychnine sulfate in that bottle," Rock said. He held up his hand to forestall questions for the moment. "Are either of you gentlemen aware of the State versus Mindit?"

I shook my head. Senator Adams said, "It was a poison-murder case."

"Yes. The law in this state is most peculiar," Rock said. "In order to prove that an accused committed a poison murder you must either show proof of the accused purchasing the poison or show him in possession of it. Our local and state police canvassed all over trying to find evidence of the former, but strychnine's too common—it's an animal poison, there's lots of it around. Briscoe could have stolen it or bought it someplace else years ago. In any case, we couldn't put him together with a purchase.

"Knowing our problem, Thurman Cartner, Briscoe's lawyer, filed a motion for a speedy trial before we did the routine house search. He hasn't availed himself of discovery, so he doesn't know about the bottle. Lieutenant Robbins, who dabbles in lab work and ballistics in addition to being our fingerprint man, assures me that what we have in this bottle is strychnine. He can't, however, qualify as an expert on that point. We do have a local doctor who'll testify the deceased died of strychnine poisoning. But the bottle was found after the fact, long after Briscoe was in jail. So I've made arrangements for a state toxicology-lab man to come here. He'll bring his equipment and testify in front of the jury about what's in the bottle."

"Maybe Briscoe and Thurman would deal if they knew about the bottle," Senator Adams said.

Rock shrugged, "They'd claim the poison was someone

else's, or that we put it in the house. What's needed is for both of you to watch the bottle. Your old friend Thurman Cartner would do anything to win this one—or any one—and you know it, Senator." He shook his head dolefully. "I was looking forward to doing battle, but I've got a gall bladder that's turned traitor. I'm due at the hospital at four this afternoon and in surgery early in the morning."

He nodded at the police lieutenant, who carefully re-wrapped his package.

"Demonstrative evidence, Robak, my boy. Trial tactics. This case is vicious but thin. We do have some evidence, but it's all circumstantial. No one witnessed the killing.

"The deceased was a man named George Wood. He was related, through his wife, to Briscoe and his sister. Edith Henzmann took his wife in when she left Wood several years ago. Time passed; things were bitter. Then Wood and the wife had a partial reconciliation. My opinion is that Wood wooed her back because she had money.

"Mrs. Wood died—she fell down some steps. Bad things were hinted about that, but nothing formal happened on it. Briscoe and Edith Henzmann both filed claims in Mrs. Wood's estate for taking care of her during the time she was away from Wood. Both won their cases. You represented Edith, didn't you, Senator?"

"You know I did. I was also asked to take Briscoe's case but decided against it. He was very angry with me about it, but he's the kind of client no lawyer needs. Thurman took him on and won his case, but not without a hard fight. Edith Henzmann got about forty thousand dollars, Briscoe only about ten thousand."

He smiled wolfishly. "High pay for house care. I don't think it bothered Briscoe much that Edith got more than he did. He ran the house they jointly own with an iron hand."

Rock said, "Wood threatened Briscoe and Edith. Briscoe threatened Wood. Briscoe and Wood had several fistfights. We've half a dozen witnesses who'll testify they heard Briscoe threaten Wood's life at various times. So we believe Briscoe took part of the poison in the aspirin bottle, ground it fine, and put it in a number of things inside Wood's house. We found it in his whiskey, in a jar of instant coffee, in the table salt." He nodded. "The liquor seems to have done Wood in. A neighbor found him long dead on his living-room floor with the whiskey bottle on a table nearby."

"I read about it in the local paper," Senator Adams said. "I had suspicions then that Briscoe could have been the killer."

"Then remember that without that poison bottle we have no case," Rock said. "So both of you watch it closely. There'll be a deputy sheriff guarding Briscoe, but keep an eye on Thurman Cartner."

Senator Adams laughed and looked at me. "Thurman has had three heart attacks and a stroke. He walks with a cane and probably ought to be in a wheelchair. But you're in for a treat, Donald. He's meaner than a summer snake. He'd try to start a fight at the Last Supper."

"You don't like him?" I asked.

Senator Adams smiled. "We once talked about a partnership, but it didn't work out." He patted my shoulder. "He's one of my closest friends."

Coger Rock nodded. "A good lawyer." He put his hand out and shook Senator Adams' hand. "The case is yours, Senator. Do with it what you will. I'll never question it."

It took the best part of two days to choose a jury. I'd spent the few days before trial interviewing some of the witnesses while Senator Adams interviewed others. It was a very thin case, but we did have evidence of the death threats and some very unpleasant photographs going for us. When a person dies of strychnine poisoning a condition usually occurs known as *risus sardonicus,* a horrible, twisted smile. The police photographer had captured that death grin. I thought the jury was going to want to punish someone for making them see and examine those pictures.

We spent the first few days after the jury was sworn getting deep into the agonizing death of George Wood and exhibiting those pictures to the jury.

Sitting with us at our table was the defendant's sister, Edith. I met her briefly on the opening day of the trial. She was a dried prune of a lady. She nodded every time a witness made a telling point for the prosecution, and frowned when a witness faltered. Her brother, Briscoe, sat on the other side of the courtroom and tried to stare her down—without success. Now and then he'd lean toward portly Thurman Cartner and whisper something.

Senator Adams went right after the case, pushing along.

Cartner had an objection for almost everything. He'd rise and point dramatically with his cane. He'd get red and angry and press his chest as if another, final heart attack was upon him. He badgered witnesses unmercifully, arguing about times and places, using any deviance he could find to confuse the jury. Sometimes the Senator rose to the bait and they'd argue cuttingly with each other.

Things seemed to go our way more often than not after the pictures of George Wood lying grinningly dead were exhibited. The judge started overruling most of Cartner's motions. But Cartner went ahead objecting. He was dogged and determined. He had a whiskey-red nose and his hair was completely white. His eyebrows looked like spring bushes covered with snow. He sat with a hand cupped over one ear most of the time. "What was that?" he'd bellow when a voice diminished.

"Why doesn't he get a hearing aid?" I whispered to Senator Adams.

"It's part of his scam. My bet is that he hears as well as he ever did. He's looking for sympathy. He wants the jury to see how oppressed he and his poor client are." He shook his head. "But he's not the trial lawyer he once was. He's lost most of his fire."

I looked at the Senator unbelievingly, but he only nodded. "He told me that this will be his last case and he isn't going to lose it."

Our last witness on the seventh day of the trial was Lieutenant Robbins. He'd brought the poison bottle. Cartner and Briscoe looked aghast when he produced it. They exchanged furious whispers.

The Senator qualified Robbins as a fingerprint expert and the Lieutenant then testified about the fingerprint he'd found on the bottle, where he'd obtained the bottle, and where it had been kept since it had come into his possession. He testified that the contents of the bottle were the same now as when he'd found it and taken possession of it. But he could not, of course, testify to what the contents were. "I move the admission of State's Exhibit M into evidence," Senator Adams said.

Thurman Cartner was on his feet. "Hold on, here. I must object. I'll stipulate, in the interests of the court's and the jury's time, that chain of custody has been established and even that the defendant's fingerprint is on the proffered exhibit, which looks like an aspirin bottle to me and was found weeks after the defendant was in jail. But no one has testified as to what's in the bottle and so its offering is premature and not yet relevant."

The Senator arose.

"I'll withdraw the offer for now and do it tomorrow through a witness from the state toxicologist's lab."

I could see that this affected Cartner badly. He took a step backward, shook his head, and sat down heavily.

The judge nodded and looked at his watch. "Nine in the morning, gentlemen." He admonished the jury not to discuss the case with anyone, pre-decide it, or read, watch, or listen to news stories concerning it, and let them go.

I watched Cartner. He was looking at the bottle apprehensively. It sat in plain view on the court stenographer's desk. Briscoe had his eye on it also.

"May Lieutenant Robbins take the bottle with him and return it tomorrow?" Senator Adams asked the judge.

Cartner objected weakly but was overruled.

We walked back to the office.

"I want you to do the direct on Edith Henzmann tomorrow," the Senator said.

I was surprised.

"You talked to her; I didn't. What should I ask?"

"I've a list of questions made out for you. I want to lean back for a time and observe things." He shook his head. "I'm getting some peculiar feelings about this trial."

I could see he was tired, but not as tired as Cartner.

"O.K.," I said. "Have you got the list?"

He reached into his briefcase and handed it to me. I read it as we walked. The questions delved into how long Edith and Briscoe had lived together, how he'd hated Wood, how many times she'd heard him threaten Wood.

The Senator had underlined the final question. "Ask Edith how Briscoe threatened to kill Wood—by what method?"

The Senator said, "Let's forget the office tonight and go get a long drink."

"Motion granted. How exactly *did* Briscoe threaten to kill Wood?"

"He said Wood ought to be poisoned like a dog."

"Dynamite!" I said. "Guilty as charged."

He shook his head, not that sure.

Just old, I thought.

Next morning our man from the state toxicologist's office was waiting in the hall with two suitcases full of equipment, ready to go to work.

Edith Henzmann took the stand. The poison bottle sat on the court stenographer's desk, tagged and ready.

I asked my questions loud and clear, fighting to keep nervousness out of my voice.

Thurman Cartner had his hand cupped near his ear,

but he didn't need to ask Edith Henzmann to speak up. If my questions were loud, her answers were louder. Her prune face was filled with outraged righteousness. Now and then she'd rub at her right ear as if it hurt or itched.

I'd figured out that in a way she was not only our best witness but also our worst. If Briscoe and Wood had feuded, then she'd been in the middle of the feud. She'd had as much motive and opportunity as her brother. I could see Cartner waiting to get her on cross-examination, writing down questions, shaking his head at the answers she gave me.

I saved the best question for last.

"In what manner or fashion, Miss Henzmann, did you hear your brother threaten to kill George Wood?"

Thurman Cartner rose to his feet for an objection. I waited him out. I watched Senator Adams, unable to read him. He sat listlessly at our table.

"Overruled," the judge said.

"Your Honor," Thurman Cartner said in a hurt voice, as if his own honor had been sullied.

"Sit down, Mr. Cartner. Your objection is overruled." He nodded at me. "Ask it again, Mr. Robak, if you desire."

Asking the question again gave extra importance to it. The judge was nailing another corner on Briscoe's coffin.

"Miss Henzmann—did you hear your brother threaten George Wood?"

"Yes. Many times."

"In what manner or fashion did your brother threaten to kill George Wood?"

She rubbed at her ear again. "He said several times that he ought to be poisoned like the damned dog he was."

"*Liar!*" Briscoe Henzmann screamed in rage. He was up and across the room in an instant.

For moments everything became a blur. The deputy sheriff pursued Briscoe. Spectators in the back of the

courtroom ran for the exits. I stepped between Edith and
Briscoe. I was too large for him to get past so he fled toward the windows, passing the court stenographer at full
gallop, overturning her chair, and knocking her to the
floor. Papers went flying.

At the window Briscoe kept right on going, smashing
through the glass. It was fifteen feet down to the ground
below, but he was already bounding across the courthouse yard by the time I arrived at the smashed window
with the deputy.

We watched him disappear into an alley while the deputy was still unholstering his gun. "We'll catch him," he
said shamefacedly as he stared out the ruined window.

I turned back. The Senator was helping the court reporter pick up papers.

The poison bottle wasn't among the papers. Nor was it
on the desk. We looked under everything. It was gone.

"He got it when he went past," the deputy said. He
nodded, convincing himself. "I think I saw him grab it."

They apprehended Briscoe later that afternoon, hiding
on the riverbank, but there was by then no poison bottle
on his person. Earlier Thurman Cartner had insisted that
the deputy sheriff search both himself and his briefcase
for the missing bottle, and had smiled tolerantly all
through the negative search.

The judge waited an hour and then declared a mistrial.
That left the state free to try Briscoe all over again—but
not successfully, of course, without the poison bottle.

The Senator and I went to the hospital that afternoon
and tried to explain what had happened to Coger Rock. I
let Senator Adams do the talking. He seemed revived. His
step was almost springy when we entered the recovering
prosecutor's room.

"The breaks of the game," Coger said philosophically
from his overburdened bed. "We can get Briscoe for the
escape and for a couple of burglaries. Maybe it's better. It
wasn't that good a case."

Senator Adams nodded. "I became somewhat uncertain about it while we were trying it."

"Why was that?" Coger asked.

The Senator said, "It could have been Edith. When she was on the stand she had an annoying habit. In the claim case every time she made up a lie or added to it she'd punish herself by batting at an ear or scratching—an unconscious thing. She did that often today."

Coger nodded. "It was either Edith or Briscoe. I'll admit I put the heat on her to testify once we found the bottle in Briscoe's closet. But she hated Briscoe. She could have put the poison in a bottle he'd used and hid it where we found it. She invited us inside and led us around when we appeared with our search warrant."

"If Briscoe was convicted, she'd have had the house to herself."

Coger nodded. "It's academic. Without the bottle, under the Mindit decision, the case against Briscoe is dead." He smiled at us. "Thanks anyway."

The afternoon paper had a big splash of a story. Briscoe was, by that time, back in jail, suffering from lacerations and a sprained ankle. He was unrepentant and not answering any questions.

I moped around the office until Senator Adams invited me to join him for drinks and dinner at the downtown Moose. On the way, he informed me we would be joining Thurman Cartner there.

I sat with them at a scarred, ancient table and tried to pace my drinking with theirs. Thurman, outside the courtroom, was a smiling, easy man. He and the Senator told stories about each other. I was intrigued by these two aging warriors, entranced by their stories of an older, easier time.

It didn't take Cartner long to broach the subject of the Briscoe case.

"I was going to try Edith on cross-examination for the

murder," Cartner said. "A mean woman. She could have done it as easily as Briscoe."

"It isn't our problem anymore," Senator Adams said. "Robak and I have returned the case to Coger."

"Would Coger still listen to you?"

"Maybe."

"Tell him I'd plead Briscoe to some small crime—burglary, escape, whatever." He tapped the table with his old, rough hand. "I thought you gentlemen had me when you came up with that bottle. I was sure of it."

The Senator stood up. I thought he looked a bit upset. He said, "I have to use the telephone."

He went and used the phone at the bar for a few moments, then walked toward the restroom. Between the day and the drinks, his conduct worried me. I excused myself and followed him.

He was standing in the deserted washroom before a mirror, examining his reflection.

I remembered his statement about ethics.

When he saw me reflected in the mirror behind him he said, "She did do it. I know that now. And Cartner would have lost this one—his last case." He looked again at his own reflection. Then he reached into his pocket, took out the bottle, uncapped it, and poured the contents into the washbowl, dissolving it down the drain in a stream of hot water. He dropped the bottle on the floor and ground it under his heel.

"I called the sheriff. I'd ordered the house searched again. They found a cache of strychnine in Edith's sugar canister."

I nodded, understanding some of it, but not everything. I'd not lived his life, but in that moment I wished I had.

I left him there, still looking at himself in the mirror. He seemed pleased enough.

Cartner had ordered a new round of drinks. "Is he all right?" he asked.

The scene inside the washroom was still with me and I

knew it would be for a long time. "I think his mirror says so," I said.

THE CALCULATOR

That was the year Cyril Ratchford abandoned practicing law until Hysell hired him for a dollar. It was a year that began badly, with Judge Evans granting a guardianship of the person on Ratchford. Ratchford felt no anger at Evans, who was an old friend. He even admitted during the judge's hearing that he had been drinking heavily since Connie had died, that his legs had recently given out, and that he'd not been eating properly—or hardly at all, for that matter.

Judge Evans appointed one of the young partners in Ratchford's law firm as guardian, and together they plotted and sent Ratchford to the Sunset Years Nursing Home. There he began to mend—or mend as much as can be expected of a seventy-year-old man with a bad liver and a problem heart.

Sunset Years was all right with Ratchford. The food was good and plentiful and his appetite returned. The attendants were friendly, although Ratchford quickly learned one didn't leave items worth stealing in view. His legs came back a little so that soon, with two stout canes and much effort, he could slowly get around.

The nursing home was full of old people and problem people, many of them forgotten or abandoned. Once Ratchford was well he soon got to know most of them and found they were people who'd lived uninteresting lives and were awaiting routine deaths. Ratchford, who'd spent his own life in deadly combat in courtrooms, found they mostly bored him.

There were minor exceptions. Down the hall there was a large old man who hit at people. He hit at attendants, nurses, doctors, and other patients—he was impartial about it. He liked to lie in wait and spring out from behind things, laughing and striking mean little blows.

The second time he did it to Ratchford, Ratchford thumped him with one of the canes. The large old man cried a little and seemed confused and hurt about it, and refused to lie in wait for Ratchford thereafter.

There was also a lady who had something growing inside her head and could no longer communicate. She talked but none of the words associated or made sense. Now and then she would stumble into Ratchford's room, fall into the lone chair, and blather away, very bewildered and earnest about it.

Ratchford found himself, more and more as time wound down for him, enmeshed in a vague ennui. He resisted attempts to get him back to the office. When he was asked if he wanted to move elsewhere he recoiled from the idea. Sunset Years was home.

He did have his guardian instruct the nursing home management that he should be allowed to wander outside by himself.

Outside was where he re-met John Hysell.

Sunset Years had once been a resort hotel-motel until cooler winters and newer motels had forced it into receivership. It had then been picked up by the nursing home chain which now operated it. Ratchford thought his firm might have handled some of the transactions.

Across the road from the rambling main nursing home building he found a path that led down between huge beach houses to the sea. Partway down the path, leading from the largest mansion—now in disrepair and seemingly abandoned—someone had built a new boardwalk continuing to the beach and terminating in a roofed lookout complete with a weathered picnic table. The lookout was open from floor to roof, but the breeze was pleasant there and the roof kept the sun from being too fierce.

So during the days, to escape the talker and to avoid the accusing eyes of the bully man, Ratchford would take a book and walk laboriously to the lookout. Sometimes he'd read, other times he sat watching the birds and the waves and the passing boats, sharing the luck of occasional fishermen and observing the beach walkers who passed.

The third time he was there John Hysell came. He came from the huge, half-ruined house, and Ratchford didn't know him at first. He rode in an electric wheelchair fabricated of shiny aluminum, and he operated it smartly. He wheeled into the lookout and smiled at Ratchford. He was carrying an ornate box on his blanket-covered lap. In one shirt pocket Ratchford spied a thin battery-powered calculator.

"You play checkers?" he asked.

Ratchford saw that Hysell's legs were useless under the thin lap blanket. His left arm was also affected. But the right arm still worked some and, above the neck, he seemed all right—smiling and waiting for an answer.

"I play checkers, chess, cribbage, gin rummy, and anything else you can think of." Connie had been a game fanatic.

Hysell's face tilted. "Don't I know you?"

"Cyril Ratchford. I am—or was—a lawyer."

Hysell nodded. "You did some work for me years back. And I built you a house. I'm John Hysell."

Ratchford remembered. Hysell had been a young, intent engineer-builder. Ratchford had later heard Hysell had made a fortune in construction and acquired a reputation as a man who did things right. He had built Connie's dream house when Ratchford could barely afford dreams, and it had continued to be her dream house until she died. In Florida, where anything built could be sold, Ratchford had been grateful.

"I've been watching you from what the last hurricane left of the balcony," Hysell said, pointing up. "I like the way you swing down here on those canes—like it was an effort but worth it. I'm not allowed out by my sweet new wife, Miss Two-Ton, but today she went to a bingo party and by now she's probably stuffed herself full of ice cream and cake. It was easy to sneak past the maid. She takes a nap every time Miss T-T goes out."

"Your wife doesn't understand you," Ratchford said, smiling.

"Very perceptive," Hysell said, smiling in return. He appraised Ratchford—the expensive clothes, the white hair. "She'd like *you*," he said.

"Is that good?"

"No, not really," Hysell said. "She has a history of not picking her males for permanence." He thought for a minute, looking away so that Ratchford could no longer see his face. "Can I hire you?"

"Perhaps. I'm still a lawyer, although I've been inactive."

Hysell found a worn dollar in one of his pockets. He handed it up. "Consider yourself retained."

"For what?"

"What I really need is someone to help me kill my wife. Would you do that? No?" He shook his head. "I shouldn't have asked. I can read the shock in your eyes."

"I'm only a lawyer," Ratchford said. He looked down at the troubled man. "I can be hired only for that kind of work." He hesitated and then put the dollar in his pocket. "Have been hired," he amended.

Hysell sighed. "I've never really understood your profession. I suppose that now if anything happened to her you'd report me, wouldn't you?"

"No, I wouldn't. Some lawyers would. It's a technical point of ethics. I'm going to treat what you told me as a privileged communication."

Hysell nodded. "Well, if you won't help and you won't tell, that puts us back into the checkers area." He handed over the lap box. Ratchford opened it and found an exquisite folding checkerboard.

"The checkers are in that little drawer. We turn them over for kings." He smiled. "I shouldn't stay too long. Next time I'll sneak away as soon as she goes. But she doesn't go often. She's the meanest, most calculating woman I've ever known. My third wife." He lost the smile.

"I see."

"I remember when we were younger you did a lot of criminal work, Mr. Ratchford. Did you ever defend anyone accused of killing his wife?"

Ratchford nodded. "Many times."

Hysell shook his head. "It's such a problem. She's big and strong. I bumped her once accidentally with my chair and she stopped me cold. I put some stuff in her wine, some corrosive cleaner, but she spit it out. She watches me all the time so I can't go out and buy a gun." He shook his head. "I used to be a good engineer. Now I can't do anything but operate this infernal chair and play with my calculator. It lowers the possibilities. So I suppose she'll just sit and wait for me to die." He shook his head. "She won't even let me live someplace decent." He looked up at the old wind-damaged house. "She inherited that from her last husband."

"Divorce her," Ratchford said.

"She told me if I try to divorce her she'll hold it up and maybe get me committed. Probably to a place like your Sunset Years. Could she do that?"

"Perhaps." Ratchford considered the ruined man before him. "Maybe even probably." He remembered the frustrating years in practice, the slowness, the frequent futility. "Getting a divorce can take a while, but Sunset Years is all right."

"I wouldn't mind that much, but I don't want her to realize it. Not too long ago some policemen came looking for her and questioned her about one of her husbands who died. I think she knows she has to treat me carefully." He looked out at the sea, a long look. "When we were married she talked me into putting a lot of things into joint title. When I die my two kids will get next to nothing.

"She put on almost a hundred pounds after I had my stroke. She can let me die, but I think right now she's afraid to do more. So she'll outwait me, if she doesn't eat herself to death. She went on a diet when I first met her. That was when I imagined she loved me. Now she picks and punishes and argues, trying to hasten me along. And she eats and eats." He shook his head, sick and bewildered. "How did a smart engineer wind up in a mess like this?"

"Why not make her mad enough to put you in Sunset Years?"

Hysell nodded and smiled craftily. "I'll bet that's where she'd put me. She's too smart to let me get far out of sight, too fat and lazy to want to travel far to see me dying. Sunset Years would be convenient." He gave Ratchford an odd, calculating look. "She'd see you there too. While she's involved in that maybe I could . . ."

All of it meant nothing to Ratchford, but Hysell had been a joy to Connie in building her house. He owed him semi-free advice and counsel for that.

"You can try," he said.

A few days later Ratchford found Hysell as the newest resident of Sunset Years, ensconced in a double room with a man named Schmidt who continually muttered terrible things about his family. Ratchford had thought Schmidt pitiful and had avoided the man's room. Schmidt's family were all dead.

Hysell smiled up at him from a bed. "She took my wheelchair away when we first started arguing, but I'll get it back. She's got some tax papers I have to sign and she's afraid to forge my signature." He nodded. "Look in my nightstand drawer."

Ratchford did. Inside was a deck of plastic playing cards and a fancy cribbage board.

"You're better at checkers than I am, but I'm going to beat you to death playing cribbage," Hysell announced. He punched some numbers on the ever-present calculator. "The odds are two to one."

They were playing that afternoon when Mella Hysell came visiting.

"Who are you?" she asked Ratchford from the door. Her face was all arched eyebrows and full cheeks, but Ratchford could see she was a handsome woman. Even far overweight she'd never be ugly—blimpish, but very pretty. She looked thirty years younger than Hysell.

Ratchford stood up haltingly. She watched him with eyes that seemed sympathetic.

"My name's Cyril Ratchford. Your husband was instructing me in a game called cribbage." He smiled at her. He'd been charming juries all his life.

"And you live here?" she asked, smiling back.

"Temporarily," Ratchford said.

She fussed around Hysell's bed, fluffing the pillows, straightening the sheets, all the time watching Ratchford.

"I brought those papers," she told Hysell in a low, intent voice. "Sign them now and I'll bring over your wheelchair."

"Bring my chair and *then* I'll sign," Hysell answered.

She nodded, still watching Ratchford, who was beginning to feel like a snake being eyed by a mongoose. "I started my diet today," she said to both men.

Hysell laughed. "I'll bet."

She gave him a baleful look. "Well, I did. And you know when I make my mind up to it I can do anything." She calculated him and the room. "Be nice and I'll bring you home."

"It's more restful here," Hysell demurred. "Or it will be when I get my chair."

"You'll get your chair when you come home."

Hysell smiled. "I'll sign the papers then too."

She smiled. "Whatever will Mr. Ratchford think of us—quarreling in front of him." She nodded at Ratchford. "He argues with me sometimes, but he knows what Momma says is best."

Ratchford smiled politely.

After she'd gone, Hysell seemed unwilling to go back to the cribbage game. He was pensive.

"Cyril," he said, "you must know some criminals. Couldn't you contact someone for me to hire? I know I can't last a lot longer."

Ratchford shook his head. "Let's suppose I did. If you made a deal, in law, I could be as guilty as you. Besides, your wife doesn't seem so bad. I think you're exaggerating."

Hysell gave him a penetrating glance. "She was interested in you, just as I predicted. By the time she sees you again she'll have checked you out. She took one look at your white hair and decided she was going to lose weight." He nodded. "She did that for me too. She was married then, to a man with a bad heart. He died shortly after I met her."

"You keep saying things like that. You talk about police and such. Are you saying she killed her last husband?"

"All I'm telling you are my suspicions. When we were married, for example, she admitted to two previous marriages. From what she's let slip and from what I've deduced since then, I've got to be at least number five or six. Those earlier husbands had to pass out of the picture somehow." He shook his head. "She's a creature for our time, Cyril. Florida abounds with old people. Mella's especially apt at caging the males of the species. She becomes impatient when she's not hunting. So I must watch myself and plan." He smiled. "One thing's for sure—she'll lose weight now."

"Many people diet."

Hysell shook his head. "Mella loves to eat. She'll lose now for one reason only. She means to impress you."

"I quite probably don't have as much time left on this earth as you do," Ratchford protested.

"She wouldn't be interested in you if you had a lot of time left," Hysell replied. "I wish you'd help me. Just a name and a telephone number would do for starts."

"I'm a lawyer, not an assassin."

"Fair enough. I'll just ask for one thing then—one favor. Show some interest in her."

Ratchford hesitated, then nodded, intrigued.

Ratchford found Mella Hysell the most direct and forward woman he'd ever known. It was as if she knew she could say whatever she wanted and that he was too much of a gentleman to argue or disagree.

Like the hitting man, she lay in wait for him, stalking him. Hysell took to sleeping away the long afternoons. That meant Ratchford must either spend the afternoons in his own room, lost in the agonies of daytime television, or go outside and cripple his way to the lookout area.

When he knew she waited for him he tried to find another alternative, but he was unsuccessful. Other than the path to the sea there was little of interest, and there was no other way to get to the beach within reasonable distance. To the north there were scores of tiny tract houses, most of them occupied by pensioners from the North. To the south there were more large homes, most of them damaged and unoccupied, then a bait store, then a boat place. Neither was a place to spend the long afternoons, although he tried, wandering north, then south.

So he went back to the lookout.

She waited for him on the unrailed balcony. At first she wore long concealing dresses. Later, as her weight diminished, she went to daring things—no bra, and finally bikinis.

Ratchford was alarmed, flattered, intrigued, and half a dozen other things all at once. She was perceptive to this, playing on his moods like a skilled harpist. If he seemed alarmed at the speed or direction of the ersatz affair, she soothed him. If he asked about her past life, she lied well. If he foresaw a dismal future, she always pictured them together in it.

"John isn't well," she told him. "He hates me because of that. He can't last much longer, his doctors say. And I need someone, Cyril. Someone like you—experienced, urbane." She'd accompany these speeches with a melting look that became more and more effective as her excess flesh vanished. Ratchford estimated her weight loss after eight weeks at almost forty pounds. It went more slowly thereafter, but she continued to lose. It was as if, knowing the strength of her web, she knew it would support only a lean spider.

Hysell watched and, after a while, laughed at Ratchford, but it was a laugh which understood and sympathized.

"Now you know," he said.

Ratchford shook his head, not knowing.

"In your practice how many divorces did you obtain for women?"

"Hundreds, perhaps thousands," Ratchford said.

"Didn't any of those women try to latch onto you?"

Ratchford nodded. Some had, and it had been an agony for him to treat them nicely. Connie was alive then and she was the only woman for him. There had been divorcees who clutched and cried and promised multitudes of delights. Some had been beautiful. All had been interested in matrimony, a replacement of the one shed in court. But none of them, not even the best schemer he remembered, had been as good at intrigue as Mella Hysell. He found himself enjoying the performance, and uncertain as to whether he was moved by it or not.

There was a sane Ratchford who stood in the shadows watching all.

What would you do with her? the sane Ratchford asked. *I mean, what good would she be to you?*

But he could dream and he was intrigued. It was as if, in what he knew to be the last of life, he was to be allowed once again to engage in a "first affair."

"How much weight do you figure she's lost by now?" Hysell constantly asked, using his good hand to doodle on his calculator. "Does she still wait for you on the balcony?"

"She's your wife," Ratchford told him. "This is embarrassing me. I think you should come with me."

Hysell shook his head. "She has my chair. She's using it to get me to come home, and I think it'll be time soon." He doodled some more with the calculator, cleared it, and snapped it off. "Not quite yet though. Tell me what you see in her."

Ratchford shook his head. "She's young. She's ardent. She has definite ideas about things. And she's vivid and handsome. Sometimes I feel as if I'm in distress and she's a knight riding to my rescue. She reverses the roles of romance."

Hysell smiled. "Those were my feelings exactly."

"But not now?" Ratchford said.

"Mella is interested mainly in the chase and the capture, not the afterwards. She'll pursue you as she chased me. Sooner or later you'll become the pursuer. Then she will temporize, demand plans, ask various conditions to prove your love. When you accede she'll marry you." He smiled. "By that time I'll be dead and you'll be the heir apparent."

Ratchford, realizing that Mella had already forced things between them close to the temporizing stage, said nothing.

"I tell her I hate you when I see her alone," Hysell confided. "She tells me to come home and look after my business. She understands jealousy." He smiled. "I'm not jealous. I'm only trying to figure some neat way to do her in before she does me in, but ideas that seem workable are hard to come up with. For her it would be easy. Too much or too little medicine, perhaps a pillow over the face or a fall down the steps—" He smiled again, more interested than afraid. "She's a lot stronger than either of us, Cyril. With your help, I might kill her more easily." He gave Ratchford an inquiring look.

Ratchford shook his head.

"Remember, when I go you'll be next."

"What if I'm not interested in her?"

"But you are," Hysell explained.

A few days later Hysell was gone. A nurse told Ratchford that Mella had taken him home. Ratchford waited for him at the lookout, but only Mella came.

"Where's John?" he asked, careful not to show too much interest.

"He's not feeling well," she said quickly. "He's failing, I'm afraid. Soon to be with me no more." She shook her head and Ratchford was unsurprised at the tears in her eyes. "Then I'll be alone."

He waited.

"It's been the story of my life. I've fallen in love with mature men. First John, then you. Now John will die and leave me." She eyed him warmly.

Ratchford, fascinated but wary, had a problem holding himself back from offering the wanted substitute.

"I'd like to see John," he said.

She inclined her head. "I know he's told you stories. I hope you don't believe them. I'll bring him out onto the balcony tomorrow so you can see him." The tears became profuse, and it was hard to disbelieve them. "It may be for the last time."

She groped for his hand and held it.

The next day he went early to the lookout and waited. After a time he was rewarded. John and Mella came onto the balcony. They waved to him, Mella enthusiastically,

John feebly. Ratchford hobbled up the boardwalk to be closer, to call out to them.

Suddenly, without Ratchford seeing why, Mella flew down, screaming, to join him, her black-and-white-print dress fluttering in the sea breeze as she fell. By the time he got to her she was dead, her eyes unseeing, her now thin body lying broken on the flagstones.

After a while John appeared on the boardwalk. He rolled down to Ratchford in his aluminum chair.

"She stopped my medicine," he said. "I think she was sure that would do it. I acted as if it was about to, but I feel all right." He looked down at her and did one more calculation on his calculator. "She'd lost a lot of weight. Just enough."

Ratchford nodded. "Have you ever told anyone else the things you told me?"

"Regrettably, yes."

"Well, tell no one else. And somehow you've picked up a bit of black-and-white cloth on the front of the arm to your chair."

Hysell nodded, his color better than Ratchford had ever seen it.

"Are you sure you're all right?" Ratchford asked.

"I'm fine."

"Certainly there's no way you could feel well enough to talk with the police about this tragic fall. When they arrive, you'll answer no questions. After all, your wife is dead." He looked at Hysell, whose good right hand was working at the nooks and crannies of the arm of his chair.

"Every thread," Ratchford ordered.

PAINT DOCTOR

The letter arrived at Henderson's law office on a dull, fall day. It was a substantial letter covered with bright, Japanese stamps. Sam Henderson took it from his secretary. When she was gone he opened the letter and found one sheet of paper inside folded around another sealed envelope. The second envelope was marked: *To be opened when I die,* then signed, *Iwo.* Henderson hefted it, tempted a little because he was and always had been a curious man and because he'd not heard from Iwo for a long time. He regretfully, finally, put it aside.

The single sheet contained only a few lines:

Paint Doctor,

I write you from a hospital. People look at me and we smile, but I know I am sick. Should I die, you may then read the letter I enclose herewith. My family and hopefully some part of my countrymen join me in thanking you for the years of life you gave me.

Iwo

Henderson read the note several times, examined the sealed envelope once more, held it up to the light, but could make nothing out, then put it in a drawer and locked it there.

He sat back in his chair, remembering, thinking back to an old, almost forgotten war.

It had been half a lifetime since Henderson had first seen Iwo, Colonel Iwo.

Then, Henderson had been a Chief Pharmacist flown to Santuck Island on a PBY seaplane to replace an independent duty corpsman who'd come down with Filariasis, so that everything south of his navel had suddenly swollen to alarming size. The plane flew Henderson in and the anonymous corpsman out on the same flight from and to Guam.

Henderson found himself being welcomed, if that was the appropriate word for it, in the steaming heat of a bomb-damaged concrete wharf by three marines—a captain, a gunny sergeant, and a corporal.

"Get the new Chief's seabag, Corporal King," the captain ordered crisply. He received Henderson's salute and wiped ineffectually at his sweaty forehead in return. "It's cooler here after dark," he apologized. "I'm Captain Azus." He indicated the gunny sergeant. "Sergeant Donnelly." He gave Henderson an intent, appraising look. "The General asked them to send someone who could play bridge. Do you play bridge?"

"I'd be rusty," Henderson said.

Sergeant Donnelly smiled. "If you can count honor points, you're a better man than the inept lad you replaced."

Henderson examined the three marines. They all looked tough, competent, and battle proven. "Third Division?"

Captain Azus nodded. "Sure. Real Jap eaters. Come on now. We'll show you your quarters and you can get settled in, Chief. The prisoners will be with you for sick call at eight in the morning. There are some things General Kershand will want you to know about our routine before then."

"Routine?" Henderson asked, not understanding.

"Yes. There's this program the General has set up. Your part in it is that if a prisoner complains of hurting outside then you paint the sore spot with merthiolate. If he hurts inside you give him two A.P.C.'s. That's all."

"Someone could die," Henderson said uncertainly, not liking the instructions.

"Several of our people did," Sergeant Donnelly said,

still smiling, but not so much now. "Eleven of them. We believe they were mostly downed flyers. Maybe there'd have been a survivor or two off a tin can that went down six months ago in the narrows. We think the prisoners you'll be treating under our orders killed those eleven." He nodded. "General Kershand doesn't want things made easy for them. And we think they're healthy enough. They get lots of sun and exercise." He smiled once more, this time without humor.

"You mean they killed our people during the war?"

"Not exactly. Say, instead, right at the end of it, executed them, Samurai sword stuff. All the bodies were found in a common grave inside the prisoners' compound. Without their heads. We're still looking for the heads." Donnelly nodded seriously. "Every time we get even a hint about those heads I go dig another hole. It's become a game. I've maybe dug fifty holes so far without success."

"I see."

"The Japs you'll be treating are the prime murder suspects, Colonel Iwo and his four top aides. Some people don't think we can break them. We think we can. We think we can get enough on them to hang them all. Our methods are our business. General Kershand wants nothing to interfere." He nodded. "God help you if you get in the way, Chief."

Henderson had two large tents, both with raised plywood floors. One was a hospital tent, the other, situated behind it, was for storage and sleeping. The hospital tent was well equipped for a corpsman on independent duty without a medical officer. There was a complete pharmacy, an autoclave, surgical instruments, and even a small, portable X-ray machine.

He settled in. He was twenty-eight years old and his enlistment would end in December. His course was set: He'd go back to the States for one final year of law school.

But first there'd be a few months of Santuck Island to endure.

Don't rock the boat, he told himself.

He began to unload his seabag. He put extra socks, skivvies, and khakis in an empty locker. Up the way, through a net window, he could see the marine encampment. It wasn't very large. Beyond that there would be the tents of the surrendered Japanese, thousands of them.

Henderson made himself be only mildly curious about Santuck Island. Since Guadalcanal he'd seen a dozen islands. Now he was tired of islands and atolls, glad the war was done, ready to go home. He'd seen good men die, young, bright men. Five Japanese prisoners meant little to him. He told himself he was only mildly curious about them because he'd be treating them.

He went through the marine chow line and stoically ate what they gave him. He then returned to his tents, unpacked the rest of his gear, and the few tattered law books he'd carried for almost four years.

When darkness came the marines came to his tent.

There were three of them again, Captain Azus, Sergeant Donnelly, and one new one. They came into the light of his tent, closing the screen quickly behind them against the darting, whirring night moths. They stomped and smiled.

"Get the cards," Azus said. "They're in that drawer." He pointed. He nodded at the man Henderson had not seen before. "This here's General Kershand."

Henderson snapped to attention.

"You needn't do that, son," the one star General said gently. "I read your records this afternoon. You were at the Canal with the First Divisions like me and Azus and Donnelly. You probably hate Japs as bad as we do." He stepped into the light. His hair was white and cut very short. He was thin and small and old, but he exuded energy. Henderson knew of him. A tough man. Mean.

There couldn't be more than a few hundred marines on

Santuck Island. Not enough for a General to command. Henderson had a moment of intuition.

"The prisoners?" he asked. "You're here because of them?"

General Kershand took no offense. "I know the Japanese. I know how to deal with them. So I was sent." He smiled. "Long days. A lot of questions, but not enough answers yet. So get the cards and let's play bridge. A tenth of a cent a point. I'll take your part if you don't trust yourself to gamble. The last corpsman didn't."

"I'll gamble."

General Kershand nodded approvingly at him. "Show him what we brought, Donnelly."

Donnelly handed Henderson a small sack. Inside there were a dozen eggs, a loaf of bread, and a quarter pound of butter.

"Put those in your reefer. After three rubbers we'll cook them up on your hotplate." He gave Henderson a grin. "The General gets you. Captain Azus and I are partners from way back."

Henderson nodded. A square table was pushed into the circle of light. The cards were dealt.

Henderson was at first nervous and cautious. He soon found that none of the other three were truly expert bridge players. They all three played similarly, wide open, psych bids, doubles and redoubles, daring leads, very cutthroat. Of the three, General Kershand was the most daring, the most unorthodox.

Henderson adapted. He had, in undergraduate and law school, played duplicate and regular contract bridge with able players. For a long time he'd teamed with a sarcastic man who was a life master and very good. The man, in their partnership, had incessantly smoked black cigars, used foul language, and been completely intolerant of error. Henderson was rusty, but the game soon returned, in all its intricacies, to him.

With only fair cards he and the General whomped the other two. Four dollars plus apiece.

Over eggs and toast running with butter Henderson asked diffidently, "I'd like to hear more about the island."

"Why?" General Kershand asked.

"Curiosity. And I have to treat the prisoners."

The General held up a warning hand. "Stay shy of it, Chief. They had no mercy for our people and now must be shown none in return. You will treat them within my rules. Soon, when there's a bit more evidence, our legal people will come in, relieve me, then fly them back to Japan for trial."

"Yes, sir. I see," Henderson said, not seeing at all.

"We've a dozen Japanese soldiers who'll testify to seeing Iwo and the rest enter into the prisoner compound the day after Hiroshima. We've got statements from two enlisted Koreans who dug the burial hole that morning. We can't yet put Samurai swords in the prisoners' hands. But one of them will break, one of the five. I know the Japs. One will want to live."

"The heads are the peculiar thing," Captain Azus said. His face was shadowed, out of the light. "No one but those five can tell us where the heads went. But soon, with luck, we'll know that also. If we had the heads, we might be able to identify the victims individually through service dental charts. We know you were in law school, and so you know it could make for an easier trial."

The General frowned at Henderson. "Forget your law school for now. Remember only that this is our business and particularly my business, son. You paint them and pill them. Anything more has to clear through me, and *it won't*. It's my job to make their lives intolerable until one of them breaks. We'll run them, grill them, run them some more. Not much sleep and not much food. And then they have the added burden of Iwo."

"What about Iwo?" Henderson dared to ask.

"You'll soon see." The General scraped at the rest of his eggs. "It's you and me against these two young bandits from now on. You're a cautious player, but a good one."

He gave Henderson an approving look. "Take more chances."

In the morning Henderson found out about Iwo. Two battle-garbed guards escorted four trotting prisoners, all of the procession quick stepping along. The four prisoners were slowed because they carried a stretcher. The fifth prisoner rested on the stretcher.

Outside the guards lined the sweaty prisoners up. One marine stayed on guard. The other brought the prisoners in, one by one.

The Japanese were short, dour men. They looked tired, ill at ease, stretched to the breaking point. They smelled of fish and sweat and dirt. None of the four who'd borne the stretcher spoke English. All had nicknames given them by the guards.

"This one's called Squirrel," the guard intoned. "The last doc always gave him two A.P.C.'s."

Henderson nodded and obeyed his instructions. He pilled two, Squirrel and Ace, then painted two, Eddie and Wing.

"You'll have to come outside for the other one," the guard said apologetically. "He won't get up so the others have to carry him." He winked. "I think it's getting to the place where they're damned tired of it."

Henderson went outside. The fifth man lay in the stretcher smiling a little, looking up at the hot blue sky.

"New doctor," he said conversationally.

"I'm Chief Henderson. You must be Colonel Iwo."

"No talking to him," one of the guards warned harshly. "He can talk to you, but the rules are you say nothing back."

Henderson nodded.

Iwo smiled even more. One thin hand unbuttoned a faded shirt, very dirty, devoid of any insignia of rank. His chest, on both sides, was painted red.

"Hurt chest," he explained. "Air raid. Your flying bastards."

Henderson bent forward to inspect. The smell made him almost gag. Iwo was gaunt and each bone showed. There was a peculiar, small lump on the right side at collar bone level. Henderson touched it gently.

"Paint me," Iwo commanded softly. "Paint me, doctor. Do your part in this slow ritual you make us die by."

Henderson hesitated and then dutifully painted fresh merthiolate over the man's upper chest. When he was done, at command, the other four, Squirrel, Ace, Eddie, and Wing hoisted Iwo and began their trot back to their compound. The trailing guard lifted his rifle to Henderson and grinned.

"Thanks, Doc. See you tomorrow."

Henderson adopted a routine. Each morning, first off, he would solemnly attend to the prisoners, never varying their treatment. Later in the day he'd hold sick-call hours for the marines. There he could use his considerable medical skills. He treated everything from persistent ear fungus and heat rashes to occasional broken bones. Only when something seemed beyond him did he consign a patient to the daily Guam plane and the hospital there.

Once, years before, Henderson had complained when the Navy sent him to hospital corps school, ignoring his legal background. It had done no good. So, that failing, he'd become expert, made the Navy way his way, and survived.

After sick call he'd loll the rest of the day away, reading books from the small camp library, or studying his few precious law books.

At nights, almost every night, he played bridge with the same foursome. To the great delight of General Kershand, despite the fact that Henderson continued to play his conservative game, he and Henderson won consistently.

Henderson would have been content except for the prisoners. It made him feel unsure participating in a nullity.

"Why do the guards bring the prisoners at all?" he inquired after a game one night.

Captain Azus answered. "Geneva Convention, Chief. Prisoners are entitled to medical attention." He smiled. "The Japs winked at it. We've learned what we're doing here from the enemy. Cruelty brings cruelty. So medical attention means what we decide, not what they expect and want."

"The war's over," Henderson said reasonably.

"Not yet. Not for those who did what was done here."

Henderson shook his head. "It worries me. I think there may really be something wrong with Colonel Iwo."

General Kershand shook his head. "He's faking and the others are helping him. That's why we make them carry him with them every place they go. Iwo presented his sword to me at the surrender, all very correct and cere- monial then. When the bodies were found he took to bed."

"I'd like to X-ray him," Henderson said.

General Kershand shook his head. "No way."

"If you ordered it and I found nothing, then that could hurt him at a future trial."

"I won't change the way we're doing things. One of those men will break if things continue as they are now. We run them and question them. They only sleep two hours at a stretch. Then we start on them again. Stop being a lawyer." He shook his head. "No way."

In deep night, soon after, there came to be a way. Henderson was shaken awake by Captain Azus.

"Come with me, Henderson. Now! There's hell to pay."

Henderson pulled on rumpled khakis and got into the Captain's Jeep. They jolted down a rusty road at an exces- sive speed and parked near a small, barbed-wire enclo- sure. Flashlights picked them up, beckoned them on.

"This way. This way."

Four prisoners, Squirrel, Ace, Eddie, and Wing, lay bloodily dead in a large single tent in the center of the enclosure. The fifth prisoner, Colonel Iwo, bled sluggishly from his wrists. Henderson ignored the dead and examined Iwo. The cuts were straight, but not, hopefully, deep enough.

"They all cut their wrists," Azus said, somehow scandalized about it. "God knows where they got a razor. We check them all the time. They passed it on, one to another. Iwo was last. Maybe he chickened out. The others cut groins too. He didn't."

"Get him to my tent. I'll sew him up and start plasma," Henderson said. "He's lost a lot of blood. He's weak and could die also."

Captain Azus nodded agreement. "The General isn't going to be happy about this. A lot of us are going to catch hell."

Henderson directed the shaken guards in loading Iwo into the Jeep. He kept pressure on the wrist cuts, stopping the bleeding. Iwo sat in the seat with his head back, looking up curiously at the night sky, his eyes open.

"Paint doctor," he said softly. "Damn paint doctor. Let me die. Then all this will be done."

"No," Henderson said firmly.

In the tent he sewed the cuts together and gave Iwo plasma, one unit, then another. When blood pressure and pulse were more normal he wheeled the X-ray unit into place and X-rayed Iwo's chest. The guards watched curiously, making no protests.

General Kershand stomped angrily in as Henderson was reading the wet film.

"Four dead men," he said savagely. "This bastard the only one left." He shook his head. "And I find you violating my express orders."

"Yes, sir. I'm sorry, sir. Could I ask you if when he surrendered his sword to you at the ceremony did he make a big thing out of it? Did he draw it, flourish it, lift it, swing it?"

"He gave it to me. That's all." The General shook his white head. "I'd put you in the brig if I had anyone else to treat this murdering Jap. I may do that yet."

"Yes, sir," Henderson continued. "I was wrong, but the pain for him must have been excruciating." He pointed at the X-ray. "His collarbone's splintered on the right side. You can see the break and the calcification around it. The edges don't meet well. If he tried doing much, even now, he might cause the fracture to compound, come through the skin. And there are, at my count, at least four rib fractures on his left side, probably more. Our last bombing raid on Santuck—was it before or after Hiroshima?"

"I'd guess before. After the bomb at Hiroshima everything stopped in this area." General Kershand drew closer to the X-ray film, frowning at it.

"This man didn't cut off any heads with that shoulder."

"This is none of your affair," General Kershand said coldly. "This man is your enemy. You're not his lawyer. Whether he wielded a sword or not, he was in command of this island. He participated."

"General, with all respect, this man will eventually be tried by lawyers, defended by other lawyers. Without someone around to put the sword in his hand or the words of command in his mouth, he's not going to be found guilty."

"Perhaps. That's conjecture."

Henderson nodded surely.

"They've beaten me, then," General Kershand said softly. "They died to beat me."

Henderson sensed the same thing. He nodded.

The General looked away and then back. He smiled sourly. "My recollection is you're due out in December, Henderson. You've probably cost yourself some added time tonight. With four dead and Colonel Iwo in the shape he's in, my job here's done. I'm going to fly back to Guam with you and Iwo." He stopped for a moment, thinking. "Maybe there'll be a decent bridge game there for an old plunger who's about to retire." He nodded.

"You argue Iwo's case with the legal people there. You show your X-rays to the doctors."

"Yes, sir," Henderson said. "I will."

"Why, Henderson? Why bother with an animal like him?"

Henderson thought for a moment. "Perhaps because what we were doing was no more right than what Colonel Iwo was accused of doing. Also, because I was curious. Mostly because he tried hard to die with the others, to cheat us also. His cuts are straight. There are no hesitation marks. He just couldn't get pressure enough on the blade to get the job done. He was so weak he never got to his groin area. Maybe the razor was dull. But if he couldn't commit suicide, he logically couldn't lop off heads with a Samurai sword."

The man on the cot moaned. They both watched as he awoke and stared about him. He pulled weakly at the bandages on his wrists, but they were secure.

"Paint doctor," he called. "Damn paint doctor."

"More than that," General Kershand said. He shook his head and went out into the night.

The obituary made the front page. It recounted Iwo's accomplishments as a Japanese statesman, as a leader of the diet or legislature, as a cabinet member. The story said the sane world had lost a sane, reliable friend. There was even, Henderson found, a long, complimentary, even flowery, editorial about Iwo inside.

Henderson unlocked the drawer and opened the second letter:

Dear Paint Doctor,

What I did, during the war years, seemed right to me then. Things I did then are abhorrent to me now.

Thank you for helping me. What your people did to me and the others attempting to obtain our confessions was also a wrong. I am glad I did not die. Perhaps I am now innocent as once I was guilty.

One of your prisoners, the last one, broke my collarbone. The rib injuries did occur during an earlier air raid.

My family died at Hiroshima. With strong drugs and hot anger all things become possible. When it was over I alone weighted the sack of heads and dropped them secretly in Santuck Bay.

Iwo

Henderson read the letter without surprise or regret. He put it back in the drawer when he was finished. A few days later he remembered it, took it out, read it once more, then burned it.

DEADLY HUNGER

They were, Bruno found, people of anger and violence, particularly Aunt Nora. They were thumpers, pinchers, beaters, living in singly held camps, sometimes together, but apart in many ways.

Ralph was mean and lazy. Aunt Nora was mean and penurious.

Watching the two of them made Bruno feel a little like he'd felt the night he'd been thrown a hundred, skidding feet from the auto crash which had burned his mother to death: unable to move, fascinated and horrified at what he must see.

If he placed an empty glass against the bedroom wall, he could hear them when they weren't running the old, window air-conditioner. He was afraid to do it often because it was an uncertain summer weatherwise. Besides, Aunt Nora could move very silently.

He heard Aunt Nora say once, "He's so damned much trouble, rolling here, rolling there. He's started eating a lot, too. Have you noticed? I should go to court for more money, but that might mean trouble." She paused and Bruno had to strain to hear. "There's his trust fund. More than a quarter million."

Ralph, out-of-work actor, husband number three for Nora, said something, but Bruno missed it. He talked softly, was huge, and now and then he'd pinch Bruno or thump him on the head, but usually he ignored him. Aunt Nora was the one to fear.

"I'll think of something," Aunt Nora said.

Bruno was twelve years old that summer when Aunt Nora came to take him home from the LaRuse Home and School.

"I'd like to stay here," he told her truthfully. "I like it okay, Aunt Nora." He'd called her that grudgingly, because the social worker had said he should. "There's a pool and a gym. The doctor said if I worked hard there's an outside chance for me to walk in braces one day."

She smiled an unbelieving, false-teeth smile at him. She was his great aunt, old, and his only living relative. He remembered his mother hadn't liked her and they'd never visited.

"I talked to welfare and they went to the judge and he gave you to me." She gave him a severe look. "You need to be realistic, young man. Paraplegics don't outgrow it." She nodded. "I'm going to take you. There's only Ralph and me. I'm semiretired from pictures. We have a nice place."

Miss Malvin, the social worker who supervised the home, nodded at both of them, her puckered face eager. Bruno was sure Miss Malvin would be glad to be rid of him. He was the only wheelchairer in the school. He'd tried not to be a problem, but by the very nature of his disablement, knew he had been.

"Bruno's self-sufficient," she said. "Give him a problem and he's very dogged and determined about it. He'll solve it every time."

Aunt Nora nodded, watching him, her small, steely eyes unreadable. Bruno tried to remember what Mom had said about her. She'd been an actress, a medium successful one, a character actress. That was where she'd met Ralph, her present husband. He was in pictures or on the stage or something. Bruno remembered Mom had shown him a squib about the marriage in the newspaper.

"He's a thinker, a planner, and a doer," Miss Malvin said. "Even boys in here for delinquency respect and get along with Bruno."

Bruno smiled. What Miss Malvin said was true. He'd waited until the largest and meanest of the bully boys was asleep and whaled him good with a two-by-four. Bruno's legs might be gone, but his arms were very strong. Now the mean ones in the school mostly let him alone. He was unpredictable. There was easier prey.

"He gets Social Security," Miss Malvin continued. "We'll have that transferred to you."

"Isn't there some sort of trust fund?" Aunt Nora asked, smiling some more, playing the kindly interested aunt. "How's that handled?"

"Now it just builds with interest and dividends. Someday Bruno will be a wealthy boy. The Social Security's enough to pay for him here." Miss Malvin nodded her head. "The trust is quite large."

"How large?" Aunt Nora asked.

Miss Malvin frowned a little, but then wrote a number on a pad and turned it so only she and Aunt Nora could read it. Bruno knew what was in the trust, so he didn't care.

"Who has the money?"

"First National," Miss Malvin said. "Everything in it is subject to court audit."

"I see," Aunt Nora said. She smiled and nodded and watched Bruno and, once again, he couldn't read her eyes.

"Home" turned out to be a hot, small room in an old house in the center of a fenced-in quarter block. The house was tree shaded, with rutted walks, plus an old shed in the back yard. The house was in the middle of a decaying neighborhood. It was turn-of-the-century built and needed paint and cleaning. The inside walls of the house were covered with photos and clippings about a younger Aunt Nora, usually in costume, mostly taken with men. In a few pictures Bruno could also recognize Ralph, a hundred pounds lighter, thirty years younger.

"Home" quickly became Aunt Nora constantly ordering and punishing Bruno. She was better at punishments than the people at the school. She had imagination. She washed his mouth out with a blistering soap, when he cursed, she beat his hands with her shoe when his bed was unmade. When he did badly she punished him. When he did well she demanded better and punished him again.

She was a woman born to command. She refused to lose any argument. Ralph was twice her size, but Bruno soon knew Nora ran the house.

She was also stingy, a collector of used twine, paper, aluminum cans, returnable bottles, and anything else with resale value. She counted her pennies constantly and be-grudged every one she spent.

Bruno moped badly at first, lonesome for the school and the few friends he'd made there. He skipped meals and picked at those he didn't skip. Neither Aunt Nora nor Ralph seemed to notice.

It was dog days summer. School was not yet in session, there was no place for Bruno to go, nothing to do. Day-time television he found incredibly stupid. Nora and Ralph watched it avidly, commenting on how good it was, sometimes playing the soap opera parts themselves.

Bruno willed himself to survive. He'd done it before, when his mother died, when he'd found out he was bound to a wheelchair. He began to eat to regain lost strength, he started exercising his arms again. As much as he could he explored his new home, sometimes secretly abandoning the wheelchair, because it left telltale marks on the rug, and crawling to something he wanted, but might not be supposed, to see. He rolled his wheelchair here and there about the house so vigorously that Aunt Nora, exasperated, ordered Ralph to build a ramp down to the yard. When it was finished she forbade Bruno to leave the yard and then let him stay outside in it all day, if he wanted. Sometimes he imagined he could see her watching him in the shadows behind the windows, her face lost in darkness. Sometimes he thought Ralph watched also.

At times Bruno thought they hated each other. Other times he wasn't sure. They had similar interests. They acted things together other than the soaps. Sometimes he was Rhett, gallant and charming, and she was a peppery Scarlett. Sometimes she was Stanwyck and he was Cooper, sometimes he Bogart and she someone in trouble.

A lot of the time they were themselves. That was when Bruno had to watch and take care.

The yard was more interesting and safer than the house. There were two smaller lots adjoining behind the back fence. The inner lot had ramshackle apartments squeezed tightly on it. Black people and white people lived in the apartments and things were loud and violent on weekends.

The corner lot had a small single-family house and a tiny swimming pool behind it. He fell in love with the pool the first time he saw it. A thin, black lady came out and swam in it now and then. No one else seemed to use it. The thin lady had two dogs she always brought with her. She tied their leashes to the diving board post and swam while they lay panting in the shadows cast by the board. Bruno watched, polite, but envious. After a time the woman also noticed him. On the third day as he watched she unleashed her dogs and walked them his way.

"Hello," she said, holding the dogs back from the fence.

"Hello," Bruno said. He moved his wheelchair closer to the fence. "Is that your swimming pool?"

She smiled, exhibiting a lot of gold in white teeth. "I guess maybe. My mamma gave it to me when she died last year."

"Could I maybe swim in it sometime? I'm a very good swimmer, but I haven't had a chance for a while."

"You're forward," she said, but she was still smiling.

"Yes, ma'am, I guess I am. But I sure do like to swim."

She considered him. "Are you related to Nora Hubler? Or has God been good and she's moved on?"

"I'm her great nephew."

"That's too bad. I don't like her and she don't like me. You can bet she won't let you swim in my pool. I had some trouble with my husband and she stuck her nose in that. He died. She stuck it into that too. She calls the police on me anonymous every time she gets a chance." She nodded. "I used to have three dogs. One of them got over the fence and now there's only two. She put poison out in your yard. Disguised it in hamburger. She got it out of your little shed over there." She pointed. "Strychnine it was. Mean and quick. I sneaked over the fence one night and found a can of it after my dog died. I called the police about it, but they never sent anyone. I've got a reputation I guess. I got sent to a sanitarium instead of prison after my husband died. The local police didn't like that." She shook her head. "I guess I'd let you swim, all things considered. I'd have to be there to make sure you wasn't going to get drowned, 'cause I'd get blamed. But Nora won't let you. You ask and you'll see." She smiled without humor. "She needs bad to die. 'The Actress.' That's what she fancies herself." She watched Bruno through the fence. Her eyes were odd, out of focus. There'd been a boy in the school with eyes like hers, a crazy boy. He'd finally run away and been caught and sent to an asylum.

"My yard's very cramped for my puppies."

"They seem nice," Bruno said. They were huge brutes. They sat eyeing him like he was dinner, tongues lolling. Bruno was unafraid. He liked dogs.

"You do pretty good rolling that chair," the woman said.

Bruno smiled at her.

"Watch close back there by the corner of the shed. There's an old well. It's covered over, but some of the boards could be rotten."

Bruno nodded. Aunt Nora hadn't told him about any covered-over well, and he'd rolled over or close to it a dozen times. *That was funny.*

"What's your name?" he asked the pool lady.

"Call me Miss June," she said, staring down at him. "Your dear auntie calls me Crazy June. The police do, too. But being thought crazy sometimes has its compensations."

Bruno couldn't think of any.

Miss June was right about one thing, though. When Bruno asked Aunt Nora about using the pool she flew into a cold, two-day whipping rage, à la Davis and Crawford.

A few days later the food war started. All that day, earlier, Aunt Nora had been very silent. She'd had her account books out, totaling figures, checking the amounts in her various accounts, frowning a lot.

She'd called Bruno in one time.

"I may need to go to court and get appointed guardian of your trust fund," she said, watching him. "Would you help?"

Somehow he knew, if he did, it would all continue on as it was now.

"I'd like to go back to the LaRuse Home," he said.

She nodded, as if deciding something. Later that day,

without reason, she stalked him and smacked him three different times.

At dinner that night she called fat Ralph a hog.

Dinner had been spotty, a tiny bread and cracker crumb extended meat loaf, some limp lima beans, and a gelatine dessert. When it was done and she was clearing the table Ralph stayed seated and ordered her to bring him bread and peanut butter and jelly which he loved.

"You've had a God's plenty," she said, exasperated.

"I'm fully grown," he said, "twice your size, little woman. I need more to eat." His voice was sweet and reasonable.

"Get out and rustle yourself up a job then. Forget the studios. Take anything. Then put something more in the pot."

"I've still got ten more weeks of unemployment left. You take the check for that every week." He waved a table knife in the air. "I want more food."

"From this day you'll eat what I eat, nothing more, nothing less." She turned to Bruno and he knew part of her performance was also for him. "Same goes for you. Eating machines, the both of you. Food costs a lot of money."

And so hostilities began in what Bruno found to be a genteel, but bitter war in which he soon discovered he was the main casualty. Breakfast became a piece of dry toast, an apple, and sweet coffee, which Nora loved. Lunch was a sandwich or a single bowl of thin soup. Supper was stringy, cheap meat, a vegetable, and water to drink.

Ralph smiled and ate the meals without complaint. He seemed big enough to take what he wanted from the kitchen shelves by force, but he didn't.

After a few days of privation Bruno found Ralph had employed other strategies.

Aunt Nora said, "Your check didn't come today from the unemployment."

Ralph smiled mockingly. "Maybe it'll come tomorrow." He nodded slyly. "You watch close for it, Nora."

She shook her head suspiciously.

"It better had. You'll eat nothing else in this house until I get that check. And you'll not use my car, either."

"I got to eat, Nora," Ralph whined. He patted his ponderous belly. "Without your car I can't go around to the studios and to my agent and I can't sign up for unemployment." He sat very straight in his chair, anger growing, getting redder and redder in the face until Bruno thought he might pop. "I got me a box at the post office. My check goes there now."

Nora nodded coldly. "Bring it here and eat here again."

Bruno had a premonition of personal disaster. He rolled a little back from the table, watching both of them, wondering whether this was a game or for real.

Ralph said, "If I don't eat then neither of you eat. I'll stay in our house and wait you out, Nora." He gave Bruno a venomous look. "That goes for the kid, too. He could go with you to court and then there'd be plenty of money. So it's his fault and your fault." He tapped his belly again. "I'll live off fat. You two won't last long." He looked at both of them hard, in what he sometimes called his George Raft style.

Aunt Nora smiled some then and Ralph finally smiled back.

"It's his fault," Aunt Nora said, nodding at Bruno accusingly. "I agree that's it. But I'll make do, Ralph."

"Sure you will," he said, lightly enough. "So will I. So be it."

Later, Bruno saw Ralph move out of the joint bedroom to the living room couch. From there he could patrol Nora's kitchen.

That night, while he lay awake and thought, Bruno could hear Ralph moving restlessly about the house, pausing here and there. Sometimes Bruno fancied he could hear the kitchen cabinet doors open and shut quietly. Finally there was silence, then snoring.

The next morning Aunt Nora confided, "He won't find anything in the kitchen. I hid the edibles in my closet when his check didn't come."

She brought him a single apple for the first missed meal and watched grudgingly as he ate it.

"You could end this," she said. "Go with me to court."

He almost agreed. Then, he shook his head. "I'd like to go back to the school."

After that food got *very* sparse.

Experimenting, Bruno found the best place to listen. In the stillness of his room, glass pressed to wall, he imagined he could hear her eating at night, her false teeth clicking.

On the second day she brought him some milk, a whole small container.

"Boys need milk," she said, not looking directly at him. She patted him gingerly on the head, doing the good mother bit. When she left he tried the milk. It was sour.

On the third day there was a single, brown banana.

He'd looked for Miss June before, but she'd been gone. On that third day he saw her in her pool. He rolled down the ramp. Aunt Nora was having her nap and Ralph sat on the couch watching him sourly as he rolled past.

He told Miss June. His stomach ached from hunger. He felt hot and weak.

Ralph had vanished from the house for several hours that morning before retaking possession of the couch.

"He's got a whole sack of groceries, mostly peanut butter and jelly and bread, behind his couch now," Bruno whispered. "And she's got stuff in her closet."

"You poor kid," Miss June said. "I could maybe call that home or welfare for you anonymous like if you'd want. Maybe they'd come out and check, maybe not." She shook her head and water flew from her swim cap. Her two dogs panted and eyed Bruno like an old bone. "That

might stop them. This time, anyway. Or you could tell
your aunt you're ready to go to court with her and then
tell the judge what they're doing."

Bruno shook his head. Aunt Nora would know.

"How about the lady that ran the home where you
were?"

Bruno remembered Miss Malvin. Aunt Nora had a
court order. Miss Malvin worshipped court orders. Besides, Aunt Nora was feeding him *some*, wasn't she. He
shook his head again. Mom's trial, where he'd gotten the
money, had taught him the law was slow and unpredictable. The school had taught him that kids died. He'd heard
a thousand horror stories, most of them true.

"I don't have my money yet," he said. "Someday I will
have it. A lot of money." He nodded at Miss June and
tried to work his way through the current insanity, forcing
himself to be logical. "Could you loan me some food?
Someday I'll pay it back."

Miss June nodded. "I can get you some, but remember
it'll be a one-time shot. If I go in and get it now, she'll
take away your ramp and you'll not get back outside
again." She gave him a wise look. "She's a careful woman,
your Aunt Nora. She wants everything to look right.
Little and thin as you are she maybe believes you'll get
sick and die and then she'll get all your money. Then their
problem, if it's real, would be over. But I've always heard
she had money. I'll bet there isn't even a problem."

Bruno had considered that before. He'd tried to find
and look at her account books, but she kept them under
lock and key. He considered it again.

Were they laughing at him, playing their hunger act
with him as pawn? They were both eating. They weren't
hot and sick and weak.

If he got sick and died she could just say he wouldn't
eat. She'd have Miss Malvin testify he'd not wanted to
leave the home. She could say things like he was de-
spondent, that he'd refused food, become ill. She could
tell them she'd just not realized how sick he was. And

who'd worry about or believe anything Crazy June said?

"First things first," Miss June said. "I'll smuggle you something out behind the shed tonight. When you come out tomorrow eat it out of sight and maybe she won't know."

He nodded. Aunt Nora would know—if not tomorrow, then the day after or the day after that. He thought some more. He didn't like life much living in a wheelchair, but the idea of dying was worse. He remembered what dying had been like for Mom. It had been heat, screams, pain.

If he survived this time then wouldn't Ralph and Nora invent another time?

Tonight he'd stay awake and listen.

Tomorrow was Nora's habitual store day.

He already knew where Ralph's cache of food was. Aunt Nora's was someplace in her room, probably in the closet, just like she'd said.

He could crawl into her bedroom so there'd be no tell-tale wheelchair marks on her rug.

She'd eat the oldest food first. That was her parsimonious way. And drink sweet, black coffee.

Ralph could be harmless without her, but perhaps not. Bruno looked toward the house and wondered if they were watching him. Maybe they were laughing at him right now, awarding each other Oscars.

Ralph too, then.

"You'd like your dogs to run over here in the yard again?" he asked Crazy June.

"Sure," she said, eyes sparkling. "Just like you'd like to swim in my pool."

He nodded and let his head hang down limply in the event they were watching.

"In a moment, Miss June, you shake your head at me. Act like you're angry and saying no to me. And then a big favor: They'd see me if I went in the shed, but when you set the food out tonight, could you go into the shed and get some of the strychnine Aunt Nora gave your dog?"

She watched him, her eyes crazy, but smiling.

"Is it quick and sure?" he asked.

"It was on Bobo." She smiled. "I'm going to be gone all day tomorrow with lots of people around so I don't get blamed." She smiled some more. "They won't ever think it's you. They'll think it's murder and suicide."

"Would a person taste it?" he persisted.

"I don't know. I don't want to know, but I've heard it's bitter. Mix it with something sweet, syrup, sugar." She watched him from a far-away place, and he smiled at her. "Then mix it with whatever."

Maybe Aunt Nora's sweet coffee? Ralph's jelly for his peanut butter sandwiches?

"A lot of it please," Bruno said, remembering Ralph's girth.

He wondered how they'd play a death scene.

WIDOW

She'd called and been sweet right after she filed for divorce. I could come any time that day and pick up my clothes. We could "talk," she said. I parked down the road out of sight and peeped under an improperly drawn shade. I could see her sitting in the shadowed front room of our tiny house. Her attitude was one of patient waiting. She was holding something I couldn't quite identify in her right hand. I rubbed the telephone wire in two.

I'm cautious. I've always been. Perhaps it comes out of my Scots ancestry, perhaps it's from seeing my parents burn in the accident where I was thrown clear. After that

I lived with my grandparents, who'd as soon waste money as words. There was no one to run to. I was too small for competitive sports. I had some late growth and am of average height and weight now, but I suppose those early years made me more of a thinker and a planner than a doer. It seemed natural to me to want to be a lawyer. Caution has aided, not impeded, my practice.

I met Janice Willingham during my second year in a Bington law firm. I was the "associate" in the office. This meant mostly that when something piddling came up one of the two partners would come to my door and beckon imperiously. I did collections, unimportant damage suits, divorces, and minor criminal stuff. It was a start.

One partner said little to me and smiled condescendingly when I ventured an opinion. To the other, the world was a plural woman. All persons were "she." If Bill Jones came into the office while I was out, this partner would dutifully inform me "she'd" been in. Perhaps a result of femlib, perhaps something else. I wondered sometimes how that second partner had lived fifty-odd years without acquiring contusions enough to break the habit. The smiler was named Connell, the gender-confuser was Guyman. My name is Sam Hubbard.

On the day Janice Willingham first came into the office both partners were out, so I got her.

She was something. I think a few like her are born each generation just to make men and women alike recognize true physical perfection. She was a trim blonde, with eyes so deep and green you could fall in them and drown. Her figure made all the figures I'd seen before seem to be totally wrong. She was wearing a simple little dress. Later, I found out the dress had cost almost three hundred dollars.

Her voice, when it came, was untutored, but soft and feminine. She waited until the awed secretary had gone out.

"I wanted to see you about a divorce," she said.

"Sit down. Sit down." Her voice brought me back to

being a lawyer. I opened my third drawer left. There, typed in bold face and taped to the bottom of the drawer, I kept a list of my state's requirements for obtaining a divorce. I thought I could now get by without the list, but this was a time of stress and I didn't trust myself completely.

"What's your name and when and where were you married?" I asked, to get her started.

Her story was old and trite. She'd married a man named True Willingham. I instantly recognized the name. The Willinghams owned the canning factory and controlled Bington's largest bank. I'd heard some about True. He was an indolent member of an industrious family. He'd never worked—factory or bank. He was much older than Janice, in his far fifties. She claimed he'd become increasingly jealous. Every glance at another person, every word she uttered was weighed and tested upon the scales of his colorful imagination.

She showed me bruises on her neck and arms from the night before. She complained he'd struck her on other occasions. When she'd threatened him with police he'd laughed at her. I was properly sympathetic and indignant.

"He told me last night maybe he'd kill me and then commit suicide," she said. A little tear came in the corner of her eye. "And he might. He's been drinking heavily. He hasn't been sober for days. I'm afraid of him."

True Willingham and family didn't worry me much. Our firm represented neither bank nor factory. I sent her to a photographer to have pictures taken of the bruises. Sometimes they come in handy in court.

I filed a divorce action for her.

All simple and routine. Except it wasn't. Not for her, and not for me, for different reasons.

All the time she was in my office I had this tremendous awareness of her. I thought she recognized it and perhaps used it. She needed me then.

On that day, after severing the telephone wire, I drove to the sheriff's office. Things must move. It was going on dusk. I wanted it dark.

"How about going out with me?" I asked Sheriff Bert Horn. "It'll be a quiet divorce. She told me to come pick up my clothes. You can be there to see there's no problem."

"Wait a minute," he said. "I'll call little Jannie and tell her we're on our way." He smiled, and I had a sudden bitter taste in my mouth.

He called, but of course there was no answer.

"Phone's probably out again," I said. "Let's take my car."

Two days after I first saw Janice, True Willingham was dead. His death caused a small furor before and after the grand jury finished its work. Poison deaths always do that.

I got the call from the sheriff's office at about three in the morning. I went right on down.

They had Janice in Sheriff Horn's kitchen. Horn was with her. A matron was pouring coffee. Janice sat in one of the straight chairs.

"You represent Mrs. Willingham?" handsome Sheriff Horn asked in the same voice that had helped him win election. I smiled at him. We were acquainted.

"Correct," I said cautiously.

Horn watched me. I could see he was testing the situation out. He said, "There's been some trouble. Did you file a divorce for Mrs. Willingham a few days ago?"

"I did. What kind of trouble?"

He held up a peremptory hand. "Let me ask the questions."

I smiled and shook my head. "Not with me, Sheriff Horn. Until I know what's going on you've gotten your last answer from me or my client if I'm still advising her."

A touch of color came into his face. "All right," he said testily. "True Willingham's dead. Mrs. Willingham tells us he called her to talk reconciliation. She visited his house. She admits they argued. She then says he knocked her around. She does have some bruises. Then he made her drink from a bottle of whiskey laced with strychnine, or thought he made her drink. He then *apparently* drank enough of it himself to kill three people."

I nodded. "They'd been having problems. I'll vouch for that. He threatened suicide."

I watched Janice. She sat carefully in Sheriff Horn's chair. Her voice was low, "He gave up on beating me. I was back in a corner where he'd trapped me, just sort of sitting there. He kept cursing me, calling me unspeakable names, saying I'd be sorry. He had the whiskey bottle, and I knew he had something in it. He poured some in a glass for me and forced me to put it in my mouth, but I spit it out when I could, when he looked away. He drank a lot of it himself and then he fell down and rolled around. After a while he quit moving."

I went to her and held her and, after a while, as if she thought she ought to do it, she put her head on my shoulder and cried.

There were a few new bruises on her neck and arms. I thought I'd seen most of her bruises before, but I didn't say anything. When she'd quit crying I left her with the matron and went into the outer office and talked for a time with Bert Horn about it. He called the circuit judge and talked with him in low tones.

"I'm going to let her go for now," he said to me. He grinned familiarly at me before we went back to the kitchen to announce it. "To convict that lady of a crime she'd have to shoot a police officer or kill a kid, and the law would need the best evidence in the world and half women on the jury."

I never forgot the words.

We were married early the next spring and for a while it was fine. I bought us a handsome little cottage in the country a few miles from town. She wanted then to be away from people. There was some acreage with the cottage, and I taught her how to fish and together we learned how to shoot. She became a dead shot.

Although the grand jury had refused to indict her the town still talked. There was money and that didn't aid in stopping the malicious stories. True's will left it to her in trust with his bank as trustee. She couldn't abide that arrangement and so she nagged me into court and I got an order naming myself as trustee. The money wasn't a fortune, but it was enough to keep her comfortable for a long time, carefully used. True had been a member of a family with money, a great deal of it, but most of it was tied up in other trusts where True's interest terminated at death. Janice didn't like that either.

"He left me almost nothing," she said to me shortly before our marriage. She looked at me with those really great eyes. "Oh Sam, what would happen if I lost you?"

I was sentimentalist enough then not to tell her the correct answer. She'd find another man.

I said, "Maybe I could buy some more insurance."

She sniffed. "I've read about insurance."

I smiled. "Remember me? I'm the lawyer. In this state for you to not be paid off on insurance at my death you'd have to be convicted of my murder. True had no insurance. If he had, you'd have gotten it, assuming the policy named you as beneficiary."

She looked a little more enthusiastic.

For a wedding present I gave her a hundred-thousand-dollar term policy and spent a couple of hours with her going over the fine print. I had to dig sometimes to make the payments.

And so we were wed.

It wasn't a long time until she was unfaithful to me, only months from the date of our marriage.

Perhaps it would have worked for us if I'd had plenty of money, but I didn't have money. Young lawyers make a pittance. I was bright enough, but lawyers make money from time spent building a practice, from experience. I was coming along well enough in the office. Small victories had made the smiler begin to ask my opinion and the gender-confuser to nod approvingly. Once the latter even put his arm around my shoulder and announced to the smiler: "She's a good boy." The year we were married they put my name on the stationery and raised my pay.

The trouble was you couldn't buy very many three-hundred-dollar dresses on my salary. She'd come from a marriage with an adoring older man who could pay the bills to a youngster who couldn't. She ran through the trust income at high speed, always behind. She was a wild woman every time she got into a dress shop. I finally called a halt to that when she was spent six months ahead. I made her take something back. It was a cocktail dress, and it had cost more than two hundred dollars. I told her adamantly she'd have to return it and earned a look that contained only hate.

It was a bad marriage for me in many ways. She wasn't very intelligent. She had a kind of inquiring look of brightness that could pass for brains and fool her admirers, but the veneer was thin. She could make a mistake, be corrected, and then make the same mistake again. Other than with clothes she had the attention span of a six-year-old. She was intensely vain. I was something she used. In her mirror there was only a single reflection. She could waste a full day trying on clothes, standing in front of a mirror in rapt, silent contemplation. She was scrupulously neat with her person and her clothes. Other than that living with her was constant cleanup. She left a wake behind her, used glasses and dishes, crumpled, bright cigarettes.

I never stopped wanting her. She was so physically overpowering that I couldn't do that. It was only that I became more fully aware of her. It was like owning a beautiful expensive car. Only after you admired the sleek exterior did you notice that the motor wouldn't start.

As I said, I'm a cautious thinker. I'd pushed hard in

school and achieved honors. I'd come to my small town of Bington for many reasons, not the least being an examination of longevity tables.

Marrying Janice was one of the few uncalculated things I'd done in my life. Sometimes I thought a part of me was standing away and shaking a finger at me even as we repeated our marriage vows.

When I was sure she was unfaithful I feigned a cold and moved into the second bedroom and waited and watched. The cerebral me was back in control.

I didn't have to wait long. The very next night she had the bottle out, a pretty party dress on, and wore a smile for me when I came home from the office.

"Cocktails and sin," she said.

I inspected her carefully. On her right arm there was a large, fresh bruise. "You've hurt yourself."

"Fell against a tree while I was outside target shooting." She held out her glass. "I'll fix you one."

"Better not," I said. "Cold's pretty bad and I'm taking pills you're not supposed to mix with liquor."

She looked forlorn and disappointed.

I tried not to look afraid.

I went on back to the second bedroom. I thought about killing her and knew I'd never manage it. I thought about her killing me and thought she probably would manage it. I thought also about the deceased True Willingham and the large insurance policy I'd bought his widow. Would she have the guts to try the same method she'd probably used on True? I remembered her making the same mistakes over and over.

I easily started an argument, then left the house.

Perhaps I could have stopped her desire to kill me by canceling the insurance policy, but I didn't do that.

The new man in her life was Sheriff Horn. I saw his car parked at the house several times.

It was full dark when we got to the house. No moon. I parked my car boldly in front. Then I led Horn up the path, staying out of the line of sight from the windows. On the porch I tapped on the door and then stepped quickly away from it.

"It's only me, Janice," I called, before Horn could say anything.

He was smiling when she began firing through the door. That *had* been a gun she was holding when I'd peeped through the windows.

I ran down the porch, vaulted the rail, and looked back. Horn was slumped against the door. He was making noises, but no words came. I wasn't sure how badly he was hit. He slid on down, and she put three more shots through the door. After the first one he didn't seem to notice.

I got back into my car and started it and waited. When nothing happened I put the car in gear and blew the horn. The door opened and she stood there looking down at Sheriff Horn. I noticed she was wearing a brand new dress—was it black?

I drove back to town, staying within all the speed laws. Both as a citizen and as an officer of the court it was now my duty to report a shooting.

PRIDE IN PERFORMANCE
(written with Eugene DeWeese)

I was leery when Chief Patch called me in. But what could he do to me that was worse than putting me on the vice squad, which is what he'd done six months ago? Anything would be better than sneaking around busting a bunch of women for making an honest—if illegal—buck or two. Patch, who still lived in the 1880s, obviously disagreed.

He looked up when I came into his office.

"Stratton," he said brusquely, "you're going out to Consolidated Electronics to help Benson."

Before I could ask if they were having trouble with hookers on the assembly lines, he had finished shifting his unlit cigar from one corner of his mouth to the other and went on. "The Stoner thing. You know about it?"

I nodded. I knew about it. Some executive named Stoner had been poisoned, right in the Consolidated plant. Strychnine in his coffee. Benson, a by-the-book type who was putting in time till his retirement next year, had been handling it.

"Well," Patch said, "things are going just a little too slow for the Mayor, who just *happens* to be a drinking buddy of Jepson, the head of Consolidated. They're afraid out there that if this drags on much longer, it could depress their stock, and it's low enough already."

"So what do you want me to do? I'm still on hooker patrol," I reminded him.

"And doing a damn good job of it, too," Patch said expansively, then leaned forward over his desk and lowered his voice confidentially, the way he always does when he wants to talk about specific activities of Vice. "In fact, that's why I'm sending you out to Consolidated. Benson—" Patch shrugged his beefy shoulders understandingly. "He's getting along in years, and he's never been on Vice the way you have."

I was frowning and pulling back from his cigar, which was deadly even when unlit. "What's all this got to do with finding out who killed Stoner?" I asked.

"It's like this," Patch said, in his just-between-us-boys voice. "Stoner was supervisor of a bunch of typists, a bunch of women, and Benson's pretty sure that one of them did it, but he can't pin down which one."

"I still don't see—" I began, but Patch cut me off with an annoyed wave of his hand.

"I just figured," he explained patiently, "that you, what with all your experience with gals down there in Vice, you'd have a better chance than Benson of spotting the ones that aren't quite telling the whole truth, you know what I mean?"

All of a sudden, I did. To Patch, women were women were women. If I was good at picking hookers out of crowds on the streets, I was automatically good at picking a murderess out of a crowd of typists.

"I think so," I said. Actually, I wasn't that much better at spotting hookers than anyone else. I just had the sort of face they trusted, so they made their offers quicker.

"I figured you would, a sharp kid like you." Patch gave me an almost-wink, then straightened in his chair and started looking for a match for his cigar.

As I drove out to Consolidated, I kept thinking about the resignation I'd typed up a month ago but hadn't gotten around to turning in yet. And about the twinges in my stomach that might or might not be the first signs of an ulcer.

The first thing I noticed about the Consolidated lobby was the poster. It was maybe three feet square and dominated the room.

"PRIDE IN YOUR PERFORMANCE MEANS QUALITY IN OUR PRODUCT!" it announced in headline-sized letters.

The uniformed guard behind the lobby desk didn't look all that proud. He stared blankly at my badge for a moment. "Something happen to the other guy?" he asked.

"Benson?" I shook my head. "No, he's busy with other things today." Like showing pictures of all the typists to the countless stores where strychnine could've been purchased. "I just want to look around a little."

The guard still looked uncertain, but he picked up the phone anyway, and pretty soon a second guard showed up to escort me wherever I wanted to go. I asked for the infirmary first.

As we walked through the large plant, past offices and manufacturing areas, I couldn't help but notice that there were empty spaces. Lots of them. The "TAKE PRIDE" posters plastered everywhere, including the empty spaces, outnumbered the people. The one I'd seen in the lobby was common, along with another showing a happy hard-hat coming out of a toothily grinning building: "PRIDE IS A FUNNY THING. THE MORE YOU USE IT ON YOUR JOB, THE MORE YOU HAVE AT THE END OF THE DAY."

At the infirmary, I got the basic facts from the company doctor, who assured me that I was very lucky to have caught him in, since he only spent a couple hours a day at Consolidated these days. Stoner had come in last Monday complaining about not feeling well, and he'd gone into convulsions only moments later. The nurse on duty—"I wasn't here personally, you understand"—was understandably suspicious and called the doctor. He called the police.

"I thought of poison immediately," the doctor said, "so I had the nurse send someone to Stoner's office to save anything he might have been eating or drinking from. We turned everything over to your colleague." He looked at me with restrained pride. "I understand it was strychnine, and that it was in the coffee cup we found in Stoner's wastebasket."

I nodded. "I don't suppose you have any idea where it could have come from? Any chance there'd be some here in the plant, for instance?"

He looked thoughtful. "It's possible. I understand they had some trouble with rats a couple of years ago."

So much for Benson and his touring picture show, I thought.

The guard—whose name was Charlie—explained about the late George Stoner as we walked. He had been in charge of a group that turned out proposals soliciting new business for Consolidated. Most of the proposals went to the government. A couple dozen people had worked for him in his department, typists and writers and illustrators.

Almost everyone in what had been Stoner's area was standing around talking.

An exception was a tiny, gray-haired woman who sat by herself with two stacks of paper in front of her and a half dozen other stacks scattered about her own desk and a couple of adjoining ones. She was apparently reading from the two stacks at once, her eyes darting back and forth. Every line or so, she'd make hasty marks in the margin of one stack.

With Charlie trailing close behind me, I threaded my way to her desk. I put on my most trustworthy face. A nameplate, being used as a paperweight on one corner of her desk, said "Martha Amers."

She looked up as I came to a stop beside her desk. "You're another cop," she said. "What went wrong with the first one?"

"Nothing. I'm just helping out."

"Do *you* think one of the women here did it?" she asked. "Your friend seemed pretty positive."

Feeling more than a little ashamed, I gave her my boyish grin, the kind guaranteed to put hookers at ease, and shrugged. "I don't know what to think yet. But frankly," I added truthfully, remembering Patch's knowing grin, "I hope Benson's wrong."

She frowned. "I see. Benson was the 'bad cop,' and you're the 'good cop.' I didn't think you people did that except on television."

My own grin became genuine at that point, and I think she sensed it.

"So," she said, "what can I do for you?"

"For a start, what did you think of Stoner?"

"Not much."

"And the typists? What did they think?"

"If possible, they thought even less of him."

"Why? He made passes at them?"

Her eyebrows went up. "Your friend Benson didn't tell you?"

I shook my head. "I'm trying to start fresh. No preconceived notions."

She watched me, some of the suspicion returning to her eyes. Then she shrugged. "As far as I know," she said, "he didn't make any passes at the typists."

"What, then?"

"You've heard of the Peter Principle?"

"You mean about a person rising to his level of incompetence?"

"That's it. Once there, he can't handle the real job, so he runs around frantically doing unnecessary, irrelevant jobs that he *can* handle."

"Stoner had reached his level of incompetence?"

"Surpassed it."

"But what does that have to do with the typists not liking him?"

"One of the jobs he was good at was enforcing every nit-picking rule he could find. And sarcastically bawling out anyone caught in an infraction."

My lips pursed in a silent whistle. He sounded worse than Patch. "Was that enough to get him killed, do you think?"

Miss Amers shrugged. "Your friend Benson thinks so. He really liked the idea when he found out it was poison in the coffee that did it, and that the typists doubled as coffee fetchers for Stoner."

"How about you? Did Stoner give you trouble, too?"

"He tried."

"And?"

"Mostly, I ignored him. Or told him off. I'm not easily bothered."

I smiled, another genuine one. It wasn't hard to believe. I looked around. "Could you explain what actually goes on here? All I've been told so far is that Stoner's group turned out proposals soliciting new business."

"That was the theory," she said. "With him out of the

way, maybe we'll actually have a chance of getting some of those proposals accepted."

"Would you care to expand on that?"

She gave me her best "you dunce!" look. "Didn't you come through the plant just now? Didn't you see a lot of empty space?"

"I noticed, but I thought maybe it was supposed to be that way."

"Hardly. We haven't gotten any new business in over a year."

"And this was Stoner's fault?"

She rummaged through the papers on one of her desks and dug out some stapled sheets. She handed them to me. "Read a couple paragraphs of this. And don't worry, Charlie," she added to the guard, who was still standing by and beginning to look concerned, "it's nothing classified."

I started reading the top sheet. After going over the first sentence three times, I stopped.

"What does it say?" I asked.

Miss Amers smiled knowingly. "You can't figure it out?"

"Not exactly. It sounds like it really should make sense, but . . ."

"That's one of the better written ones, too," she said, leaning back in her chair. "And that's just the introduction, not even the technical part. It's supposed to explain what we're trying to sell—in layman's terms. Now I ask you, would you buy something from a company that had written that?"

I had the feeling that I was receiving her favorite lecture. "Maybe the people it's sent to can understand it," I said.

"Don't kid yourself. I've heard some of the questions we've gotten back from potential customers."

"Who'll take over now that Stoner's gone?" I asked.

"Joe Anderson, according to rumor. He used to have

most of the group before he got booted into another department."

"You said 'booted.' By Stoner?"

Miss Amers shrugged again. "Probably."

"Anderson, you said. How did he take the booting?"

Her eyes met mine. "Not badly enough to kill Stoner, if that's what your unsubtle line of questioning is leading up to. Besides, Anderson would have stomped him, not used poison."

"You know anything about strychnine?"

"Where I was brought up, everyone knew what killed rats," she said, with a straight face.

"You ever see any of it around here?"

"Not personally. There were some rats—four-legged variety—down in the storeroom a few years ago, and I understand that's how they got rid of them. Pretty smelly till they found all the bodies."

"How do you suppose the poison got into his coffee? I imagine it would be a lot to expect that you saw who put it there."

She nodded. "Quite a lot. But anyone in the plant could have done it. The coffee comes from a machine out in the hall."

"He didn't bring his own?"

"No way. That was one of Stoner's favorite rules. Nobody was allowed to bring a percolator. Or even a thermos." She laughed briefly. "How about that? One of his own stupid rules helped get him."

I looked around the room again. "How about the men? What do they do?"

"Mostly look innocent, according to your friend Benson."

"They're mostly writers," Charlie the guard spoke up.

Miss Amers laughed again. "That's what their job classification cards say. Technical writers, which, theoretically, means they write about technical things. But don't bet any money on it."

"So, if they don't write technical, what do they do?"

"The only writing they've done recently has been on the slips they make up for the baseball pools."

"But the proposals . . ." I waved a hand at the stacks of paper.

"Mostly done by engineers, planners, and God knows who else. All the other departments give our group their 'inputs,' and the writers, to quote their job descriptions, 'assemble them into a coherent whole.'"

"Just assemble? What about rewriting?"

"Not if you worked for Stoner."

"So they actually did what?"

"As I said, 'assemble.' Put numbers on pages and paragraphs, make out a table of contents, that sort of thing. Oh, once in a while one of them would get a burst of ambition and repair some punctuation or grammar."

I shook my head. "You're saying they didn't do much of anything."

"Precisely. The typists ended up taking care of spelling and punctuation. And the proofreader—that's me—usually does a fast edit on final copy."

"Stoner wanted it that way?"

She nodded. "Exactly. He was an engineer of some sort, and language was beneath his dignity. Some of the so-called writers he dragged into the group were engineers, too. The real writers learned not to fight the system. Or quit."

"Any motives amongst the 'so-called writers'? That you'd know of?"

"Not unless they were annoyed because they had to goof off most of the time. Frankly, it would drive me up the wall, but it didn't seem to bother them very much."

I was silent a moment. "Tell me," I said, "just hypothetically, you understand. If you *had* seen someone put the poison in his coffee, would you tell me?"

She tapped her pencil thoughtfully. "I don't know. But I rather doubt it."

"And the others?"

"Some might. I don't know."

A whole office conspiring to kill the boss? It didn't look hopeful. While I considered the idea, Miss Amers glanced at her watch. "This job is due out today, murder or no murder," she said, suddenly impatient. "Now if you don't have any more really trenchant questions, why don't you go pester someone else?"

I took her advice and, shadowed by Charlie, made my way to a group of men clustered around a desk not far from what had been Stoner's office. I went through my "good cop routine," as Miss Amers had called it, and ingratiated myself in near record time.

Surprisingly, they didn't disagree greatly with anything Miss Amers had said, except that a couple of them were rather defensive about their job descriptions. One of them, a small, solemn man with curly hair and glasses, used words like "coordinate" and "quality control" and "time phase," which made it sound a little more dignified. Or pompous.

"How'd you get along with Stoner?" I asked when the explanation sank.

A couple of them shrugged. "Easy enough to work for," a thin one said.

"As long as you weren't female," the curly-haired one said. "He hated women and gave them a hard time on general principles. But I don't think any of them killed him," he added hastily.

"And none of you did, either, of course."

"Of course," a short, balding one said.

"You were mostly engineers, I understand. How did you get into Stoner's group?"

The balding one shrugged. "Things got slow. It was this or out the door. And it didn't work out all that badly." He grinned, looking around at the group. "The work's easy enough, anyway."

"You all feel that way?"

One by one they nodded or shrugged.

After a few more pleasantries about the joys of goofing off, I went over to the desks of the two men I'd noticed while talking to the others. They were the only ones who had stayed at their desks the whole five or ten minutes and hadn't dropped in for a word.

One, according to the nameplate on his desk—almost as cluttered as Miss Amers'—was Mike Decker. He was middle-aged, slightly on the heavy side, with a no-nonsense crew cut and a tie at half mast. An ancient typewriter sat on the flyleaf of his desk, papers around it. Mike stared fixedly at the typewriter, typed a few words. When he reached the end of the line, he noticed me standing there.

"You're Mike Decker?" I asked.

He leaned over the desk, peered at the nameplate, then flopped back in his chair and nodded. "Apparently. And you?"

I explained.

"God!" he said. "Stoner again! Look, just to save you time, I think he was an idiot and he was well on his way to ruining the company, but I didn't kill him."

"What was so bad about him?" As if I didn't know.

"As an engineer, maybe nothing. As a writer—forget it! He wouldn't know an independent clause if it bit him, and they often did. And he wouldn't care if he *did* know."

"But if he was an engineer—"

Mike snorted. "That's no excuse. I've got a degree in electrical engineering myself. Being an engineer doesn't mean you have to be an illiterate. And be proud of it, to boot."

"Sounds like a strange choice for this sort of job."

"Anywhere else, maybe, but not here. The president of Consolidated is an engineer. And so are most of the brass."

"And they thought Stoner was doing a good job?"

"Apparently. They can read this crap and understand it," he said, gesturing at a pile of papers at the back of his desk. "So they can't believe that it isn't crystal clear to our potential customers."

"Couldn't you have rewritten it?"

Mike snorted again. "Under Stoner we were allowed

only the most minimal of changes. He was afraid the sacred technical content would be changed if we got too wild in rewriting."

"If you don't rewrite, what's this?" I asked, looking at the half-filled sheet of paper in his typewriter.

Mike laughed. "This has nothing to do with Consolidated. I do some free-lancing, mostly for trade journals."

"You write the articles here? On company time?"

He shrugged. "It's better than thumb twiddling or bull shooting, which are the only other choices."

"Didn't Stoner object?"

"All he cared about was getting his pages numbered right. And making sure nobody changed his 'technical content.' That doesn't take much time, and Stoner, believe it or not, never let anyone work on more than one job at a time. Do you have any idea what that means? Aside from letting Stoner keep ten writers on the payroll instead of two, which are all it would take to do what he wanted done."

It sounded as bad as a stakeout. At least in Vice you kept moving and met interesting people, even if you didn't make any firm friends among them.

"And that's all he ever let you do?" I asked.

"Just about. Oh, we'd get some extra assignments now and then from outside the department. Those cruddy posters, for instance." He waved at one pasted on the far wall. This one I hadn't seen before. It showed the same happy hardhat, but this time he was standing next to a production line. He had one foot lifted, bringing it down in a stomping motion. A small, bug-like creature right out of a Raid commercial looked up in horror at the descending foot. "TAKE PRIDE IN YOUR WORK," the caption read. "HELP STAMP OUT DEFECTS!"

"You did those?"

"Carl and I worked on them," he said, gesturing toward the one other man who had stuck to his desk. "It was mostly for laughs, considering the way things are going around here." He shrugged. "But maybe things will change now. And I'll have to do my free-lancing on my own time."

Charlie the guard, I noticed, had dropped out of my parade at the last stop and was still shooting the bull with the writers a half dozen desks away. I wished Mike luck and approached the Carl he had pointed out.

The nameplate said the full name was Carl Billings. Like Mike's, Carl's desk was a sea of papers, but neatly stacked ones. Along the back of the desk, next to the file basket, stood a dozen blue-covered books. They reminded me of the workbooks I'd had in high school and college.

Carl was oblivious to the hubbub in general and me in particular. He was reading the top paper in one of the stacks and was, slowly and deliberately, crossing out entire lines and replacing them with one or two words. He was a little younger than Mike, fifty pounds lighter, with blond, thinning hair and an apologetic face.

"Mr. Billings?"

He blinked through his glasses as he looked up at me. "Yes?"

I introduced myself and my badge. For a change, he didn't want to know what had happened to Benson. On the other hand, he agreed with Mike that the typists, despite excellent motives, had surely not killed Stoner.

"I take it you didn't care much for him yourself," I said.

"You take it correctly. He was a most unpleasant person. But I'm sure things will change now." He tapped the stack of papers he was marking up. "We might even turn out a proposal someone will understand." He smiled faintly.

"What did you do before you got shanghaied into Stoner's group? Assuming you were shanghaied, that is."

He nodded. "I was. No one in his right mind would come to work for the man voluntarily. I worked mostly on maintenance manuals. Except last year, when I did these." Billings gestured at the blue-covered books on his desk.

I picked one up and glanced through it. It was constructed a bit like those old Big Little Books, with a hundred words or so on each left-hand page and an illustration on each right-hand page. The one I was looking at was a simple explanation of basic electronics. So simple even I could understand it. It was as far removed from the stuff Miss Amers had showed me as I could imagine.

"You did this?"

He nodded, waving at the books. "All of them."

"It looks a little elementary," I said, "particularly for a company full of engineers."

He smiled again. "Stoner practically had apoplexy when he saw it. But that's what the customers wanted, and those were practically the only things we made a profit on last year."

"But while you worked for Stoner, you did what the rest of the writers did?"

His face lengthened. He nodded, then looked down at the marked-up paper he was working on. "Things will change now," he said.

And so it went for the rest of the morning. To make Patch happy, I took a couple of hours to do some formal questioning, trotting everyone into a nearby conference room one at a time. Needless to say, no one broke down and confessed, and, despite Patch's confidence in my ability to detect hookers, liers, and/or murderesses, I didn't detect anyone in any of those categories. Or murderers, either, for that matter.

At noon, Charlie and I picked up some sandwiches in the cafeteria despite Miss Amers' warning to steer clear of cafeteria food. After lunch, I got the personnel files from a very offended-looking secretary. "Officer Benson has already seen these, so I do not see why you need to paw through them, too." She eventually gave in grudgingly, and Charlie and I took them back to the conference room we'd used for the formal questions.

There was nothing spectacular in any of the women's folders. Stoner had given them all generally average marks except for Miss Amers, who got a grudging "good" in a few categories. Her previous supervisors, however, had been practically ecstatic.

The engineer-writers fared no better. Stoner's evaluations were middle of the road. A couple of them got low marks for punctuality, but that was about the sum total of the variations. Their earlier evaluations, when they'd been classified as engineers, had been fairly routine, too. Most of them had put in a lot of years with Consolidated, apparently never doing anything more exciting than getting ten-years-of-service tie clips and going out for the department bowling or softball team. None of them seemed to have ever made any complaints, however. Nor had they since they'd been transferred into Stoner's group. None had asked for a transfer or anything.

This was in marked contrast to the women, all of whom —except for Miss Amers—had asked for transfers within a few weeks of getting into Stoner's group. I could imagine his reaction to the requests, so it was no surprise that none of them ever asked twice.

Then there were the two writer-writers. Mike Decker's earlier evaluations had been better than average but not spectacular. Fair command of English. Excellent technical knowledge. About average in the everpresent "pride in performance." From Stoner's evaluations, however, you couldn't tell Mike Decker from any of the others. Average everything, even punctuality.

Carl Billings, on the other hand, had gotten excellent evaluations from previous supervisors and an extremely poor one from Stoner. Extremely conscientious, very high in "pride in performance" said the earlier ones. Not exceptionally productive, but what he did turn out was good. There was a special commendation for the basic electronics texts.

His evaluation from Stoner was just the opposite. Poor attitude. "Attempts to assume excessive authority." I assumed that meant that Billings had made the mistake of trying to do some rewriting and had disturbed Stoner's technical content. Like the typists, Billings had requested one and only one transfer almost immediately after getting drafted into Stoner's group. And there was a medical notation, something about an ulcer flare-up. I smiled sympathetically.

By midafternoon, I was ready to throw in the towel. I was going over the same ground for the third time, and Charlie was getting twitchy just sitting around watching me. Nothing had leaped out at me, either from the people's faces or from their personnel files.

At least, I thought, as I gathered up the files and headed back for Personnel with Charlie, I hadn't come up with anything to point to any specific typist the way Patch had hoped. And unless Benson found some clerk who would swear that one of them had bought some strychnine, there never would be anything.

We were half way from Personnel to the lobby when my name came over the plant's P.A. system. I had a phone call and I should pick up the nearest phone and call the operator. Charlie pointed out a phone, which I reluctantly picked up.

It was Patch, of course. He wanted to know if there had been any progress. Had I spotted the hooker in the woodpile, so to speak. When I told him no, and that I didn't think any of the women had done it, he laughed crudely.

"Come on, Stratton! Take another look. I told you, you do a damned good job in Vice, so just do the same job there. Don't let them fool you. Just because they're dressed a little classier and they pound a typewriter for a living doesn't mean they're any different underneath. You know what I mean. Now give it another try, okay? Before Jepson gets the Mayor on my back again."

Before I could do more than sputter angrily, he'd hung up, which was just as well. I stared at the phone for a while, thinking once again of my as yet unused resignation and the maybe-ulcerous twinges I was getting again. Finally, I nodded to Charlie and we started back toward

Stoner's area. And as we walked, visions of Patch still flitting in front of my eyes, one of the ubiquitous posters suddenly leaped out at me. I'd seen it before, but this time, with the twinges in my stomach getting sharper, I saw it a little differently. I stared at it for several seconds, an idea bobbing to the surface. It wasn't a great one, but it was all I had and was worth a try. Although, looking back, I almost wish I hadn't made the try.

Back at the scene of the crime, things seemed busier. Only a few people, mostly the writers, were standing around talking. And a man I hadn't seen before was in Stoner's office. Anderson, I assumed. Mike Decker and Carl Billings were both in the office with him, along with a couple of the other writers.

I waited until they came out, each with a sheaf of papers. I caught up to Billings at his desk.

"Things back to normal?" I asked when he looked up. "Now that Anderson's taken over again?"

Billings said nothing, only nodded. I noticed out of the corner of my eye that Miss Amers was watching me suspiciously, maybe a little apprehensively.

"Working for Stoner must have been tough. These books, for instance," I said, tapping the blue-bound volumes. "You couldn't have done anything like that in Stoner's group."

"Probably not. He would've found some way of stopping it."

"And having to work—or not work, actually—on those proposals."

Billings nodded again. He looked as if he were waiting for something from me.

I gave it to him, almost hoping nothing would happen. "It wasn't any of the women who killed him, you said so yourself. It wasn't any of the other writers. Most of them were happy doing nothing and getting paid for it. And Mike was content doing his articles on company time and getting paid double for them. But you—you took those posters you and Mike made seriously. You took pride in what you did, and Stoner wouldn't let you do it any-more."

I waited, still hoping. Miss Amers was now definitely watching with apprehension. If anyone knew the truth, it was her.

Finally Billings sighed. "Am I under arrest?"

Reluctantly, I nodded and read him his Miranda rights. "You admit doing it? Poisoning Stoner?"

Another sigh. "He deserved it, didn't he?"

I didn't argue. I stepped back, waiting patiently while he slowly put the cover on his typewriter, pushed back his chair, and stood up. We walked across the room and past the poster that had given me the idea—the one showing the happy hardhat stamping out the defect.

Billings held himself erect. I saw—or thought I saw—a faint look of pride on his face, and I wondered how his ulcer was doing lately.

And in the bug-eyed defect on the poster, I saw Chief Patch's face.

It was something to think on.

FIFTY CHINESE

My law partner, the Senator, said in a reasonable voice, "You can't get a change of prosecutor, Robak."

I nodded, knowing that. Under our state's rules of procedure, where you allege bias, you can get a change of judge in a criminal case, but the judge wasn't our problem. The prosecutor, Timothy Toy, was.

"I know it's not the law, Senator." I frowned and gave him back one of his own favorite sayings which he sometimes used when things weren't legally going his way. "But it ought to be. There's truly a great need for it."

We were sitting in the Senator's office and discussing the upcoming murder trial of Richmond Clement.

"First time I ever heard of a defendant passing a lie detector test and the prosecution not giving it any credence at all," the Senator mused, somewhat scandalized. "It sort of shakes your faith in the system."

I brooded about that for a time on his old leather couch while he went back to reading something in *Corpus Juris Secundum.* In many ways he was a disorganized man. Books were piled in corners, stacked high on his desk, shelved in a disorderly fashion, and even in half a dozen messes on his floor. It wasn't that he was a careless man. Like someone who has taught the first grade for fifty years, he knew. It was only that he never seemed to complete a job of research.

Outside it was the cold of mid-winter. The jail had been chilly when I'd visited there half an hour before.

I'd also earlier argued a motion in *limine* in Judge Steinmetz's court, a motion filed by the state. The motion was to keep me from mentioning, in any fashion, the results of any lie detector tests, asking any questions about any lie detector tests on *voir dire,* or of any witness, or calling any polygraph expert.

Within me was the sinking feeling that the good judge, who knew the law, would grant the state's motion in due time.

The Senator looked up from his book and became aware I was still there. "Tell me again what they've got in the way of evidence?" He leaned back in his old chair and grinned at me through yellowed dentures.

"No direct evidence except the one eyeball witness. Richmond Clement and the deceased were two of a kind, both of them cantankerous and mean. They owned adjoining farms and there had been several boundary disputes, some fence repair arguments, and general acrimony ever since they became neighbors ten years ago.

The deceased was Howard Ryan and he was married, prior to his demise, to the good prosecutor's great aunt, Lara Toy Ryan. Mrs. Ryan says she watched Richmond Clement come onto the Ryan property, saw him argue with her husband, and then saw him shotgun Ryan down with a twelve gauge belonging to Ryan which he conveniently kept in his barn." I nodded, remembering. "There are some very ugly pictures."

"Fingerprints?"

"None. Richmond was arrested and immediately claimed he'd not done it. I arranged a lie detector, and he passed it." I smiled. "Thereafter we offered to let the state police test him with both sides being bound by the results and Toy declined. Says he doesn't believe in polygraphs any more."

"Could the wife have done it?"

"Anyone could have. Ryan wasn't a gentle man. Any passer by, any wandering stranger, any old enemy could have done it. Richmond claims, and I feel, that he's just the most likely suspect, so Mrs. Ryan picked him. He has no alibi. And she hates him, mostly because her husband hated him I'd guess. She's an old lady. I took her deposition and got lots of sighs and tears and venom."

"Smoke screen?" he asked.

"Perhaps. I don't know."

"I've known the Toy family around this town and county for all my life. They usually live to be ninety or a hundred years old. As a family they share certain traits, they're all mean and they're all vengeful. I'm sure you've had enough problems with the prosecutor to agree with that?"

I nodded. He could be right, but Lara Toy Ryan had moved like a careful old dog out for a stroll the day I'd deposed her. And all I'd gotten deposing her was of no value.

"What else?" he asked.

"There are maybe a dozen witnesses to the Clement-Ryan arguments and threats. Our man drinks a bit. He'd threatened to shoot Ryan in a lot of area bars." I nodded. "I told Toy I'd plead Richmond guilty to having a bad temper."

"How about her eyesight?"

"That's one bright thing. It's only fair. She wears glasses and had a cataract removed from her right eye a year ago. Her eye doctor slipped me the word that she sees pretty well with her glasses when she wears them. He didn't know if she wore them all the time." I thought for a moment. "My bet is she'll swear she had them on whether she did or not. I wondered a little, during her deposition, whether she ever really saw anything at all?"

"Hmmmmmmph," Senator Adams said, clearing his throat and looking out his fogged window. Now it was snowing. He took off his own glasses and polished them with a frayed handkerchief. He wasn't a very neat man. "When did this murder supposedly happen?"

"Last October. No tracks in or out, a dry cool day." I shook my head, frustrated. "So my man says he didn't do it, takes a polygraph and passes it, and is still on the hook because he's all the prosecutor's got. Besides, Toy's dear uncle is dead and his aunt teary eyed and vindictive."

"Did Clement do it?"

"He says not."

"Has he paid us?"

"Adequately if not munificently. He put a mortgage on his farm to come up with the money." I struck my palm with the fist of my other hand. "What we have is one mean, nasty old defendant as our only witness."

"Married?"

"Divorced. A long time ago."

"Has the prosecutor made you any offer?"

"Thirty years. At Richmond's age that would be life for him."

"Well, it does sort of shake your faith in the system," he said again. "Let me think on it overnight and we'll talk some more tomorrow." He looked up at me keenly. "Are the sheriff and the prosecutor still on the outs?"

I nodded. "Yes, sir. That's my only source of encouragement. The sheriff looked over the jury list with me. And he kind of likes Richmond for some reason I can't fathom."

"The story I hear is that Prosecutor Toy is backing the sheriff's chief deputy for the office in the upcoming spring primary."

"Yes. That's why they fell out."

He tapped a gnarled, old finger against his desk top. "Did you ever hear me tell the story about the fifty Chinese?"

He had a thousand stories. Some of them I'd heard many times, but I didn't remember a Chinese story. I shook my head resignedly.

"I'll tell you about it later," he said, perhaps reading my mood. "Richmond Clement has some brothers around here, doesn't he?"

"Yes, sir. Two of them. One's six years older and lives here in town. The other is four years younger and lives next county north."

"Have you seen them?"

I nodded.

"Would they resemble Richmond?"

"There's a strong family resemblance. The older brother would outweigh Richmond thirty pounds, the younger one is Richmond's build, but maybe three or four inches shorter."

"Chinese," the Senator said softly. He looked down at a turnip watch. "It's time for me to retire to the downtown Moose for Bourbon and branch. Join me? We'll think some more on this."

"Not tonight," I said. "I guess I'll look over instructions and try to dig out some more good law on motions in *limine*."

"You'd do as much good drinking Bourbon and branch," he said, grinning again through his dentures.

I shook my head.

"One more thing then. Did you check to see if Mr. and Mrs. Ryan were getting along in their marriage?"

I nodded. "I couldn't find anything to indicate otherwise. Still I'll whack her with that on the stand if I think there's any chance to create confusion. She came over very meek and surprised and tearful and mad on the deposition."

He nodded. "Cunning. Toys are mean and cunning." He shook his head. He didn't like Prosecutor Toy any better than I did.

In the morning I had an early surprise. Richmond Clement's two brothers awaited me at the office.

"Senator Adams called last night and asked us to come in early," the younger one, Arthur Clement, said. The older one, William, nodded stolidly.

Virginia, our peerless secretary, shook her head. "He's not in yet." She gave me a nasty look. "And if you don't stop getting him into criminal cases at his age, the day'll soon come when he doesn't make it in at all."

I nodded contritely. If there was a pecking order in the office, it started at Virginia, then moved on to the Senator, then lastly to me.

"I didn't even know he'd asked these men to come in," I mumbled. I was saved from further secretarial harangue by the arrival of the Senator. He was freshly barbered for a change and he had a man with him whose face was vaguely familiar.

"You men come into my office," he said.

Virginia frowned at her exclusion and went back to her typewriter, pounding it savagely.

"This is Lester Shay," the Senator said, introducing his companion. "And these are the brothers of the man I just showed you in the jail. This, of course, is my young associate, Don Robak."

"You run a local beauty parlor," I said brightly, remembering his name and face from somewhere.

"Lester does a bit more than that," the Senator said.

"He's a cosmetologist and a barber and more. He worked for a while in New York at one of the theaters there doing make-up and the like. He's the make-up man for the River Players group locally. He's as close as we'll get in Bington to what we need."

Lester smiled conspiratorially, still sizing up the two Clement brothers. "Close enough, I hope."

"Can you do anything with these two?"

"I can try. There are possibilities."

"You're going to try to make them up to look like Richmond?" I asked.

"Not exactly," the Senator said. "I do have an immediate task for you. I'd like you to seek private conference with Judge Steinmetz. Tell him I'm into this with you. Try to get him to trade your loss of the motion in *limine* for the right to have these two brothers kept and brought from the jail during the trial each day with Richmond. You can tell him the sheriff has approved it. If I know Steinmetz, he'll be upset at Toy keeping your polygraph testimony from the jury. So we'll give the prosecuting witness a line-up she can truly pick from."

I inspected the idea for flaws. "The chief deputy will surely know which one Richmond is. He'll tell Toy and Toy will tell her."

"Of course that will happen," he said. "The prosecutor is a devious man. We'll do some sleight of hand, Donald. The sheriff knows about that, too. He's enthusiastic about it."

I nodded. "I've got it. The sheriff will send the chief deputy somewhere else on business or maybe vacation?"

The Senator shook his head. "Wrong." He smiled. "Let me do it my way."

"You're going to take over the trial?" I asked.

"Let's say, instead, that I'm going to sit beside you while the trial is happening."

We began trial the following Monday morning. If Prosecutor Toy was dismayed when the sheriff brought over three defendants instead of one (Judge Steinmetz having agreeably consented), he gave no sign. He nodded at the chief deputy, who nodded back and, I thought, winked, and then began to wrangle with me about the jury selection.

We had a jury by noon.

I tried then to do my usual job. I was persnickety and contentious. I acted like a pup at a bird hunt. I objected to exhibits and questioned relevance and materiality. I doubted chain of custody. The Senator sat next to me, smiling and nodding. After all, he'd taught me. On the other side of the Senator sat the three brothers, also smiling and nodding, as if on cue from the Senator.

The rules of evidence are complicated, but Prosecutor Toy had done his homework well and he won most of the important arguments. I did manage to harry him into anger a number of times so that his perpetual courtroom scowl grew steadily deeper.

I knew, of course, which of the three my client was. If he'd been tampered with in any fashion by the Senator's make-up man/beauty operator, I could see no evidence of it. He had been instructed to smile instead of frown, but I'd done that early.

The younger brother, Arthur, had been extensively made up. His hair had been cut short, his eyebrows plucked down thin, and the Senator must have instructed him to frown instead of smile. It also seemed to me, when they brought him and removed him with the other two, that he was taller.

Prosecutor Toy showed the jury his inflammatory photos of a man shot in the head at close range by a shotgun. Steinmetz kept out the color photos, but let in black and whites. Toy paraded the death shotgun in front of the jury time after time, passed clear plastic envelopes containing buckshot extracted from Ryan, let them dwell for almost a day on the testimony of a doctor who described in fearsome detail what had caused Ryan's death. Then he had them listen to ten different witnesses testify to overhearing Richmond Clement threatening Ryan at various times.

It became obvious, after a time, that Prosecutor Toy was saving Mrs. Ryan as his final witness, to tie it all together by identifying Richmond Clement as the man who'd done the killing.

"Watch the time," the Senator said anxiously to me. "When Toy's done with her I want to be able, under the right circumstances, to forego most cross examination and go right to our case."

"How do you mean?" I whispered back, puzzled.

"I don't want them to finish with her in the late afternoon so we then have to wait until next day. I want her to make her identification and then us go on right then." He smiled at me. "You know which one Richmond is, don't you?"

"Sure. You didn't change him any."

He smiled mysteriously and I was momentarily unsure. I looked down the row of three and was sure again.

The Senator was getting up in years. I sighed to myself. Maybe a touch of senility.

They put Lara Toy Ryan on the stand as the first witness on the sixth day of the trial. She had a high-pitched voice which I remembered, but she seemed stronger than when I'd deposed her. I wondered again, as I had before: Could she have killed her husband?

It became obvious early she was out for Richmond's blood.

"I saw it all. My husband never had a chance," she wailed.

I objected and had it stricken and the jury admonished, but I knew that what she'd said, like the ghastly photos, had made an impression on the jury. They seemed to me as if they were only waiting for their time to come so they could dash to the jury room and convict Richmond Clement.

Toy said, "And now, Mrs. Ryan, we have reached a

point in the trial that all of us have been waiting for anxiously. Please look over at the defense table."

She did.

"Notice that defense counsel have three men seated beside them in an obvious effort to cause you identification problems. Is there a problem?"

"No, sir."

"Do you know which of those three men shot and killed your husband?"

"Of course I do."

"Do you see all right, Mrs. Ryan?"

"With glasses my vision is close to normal. And I was right up there at the window watching from behind the curtain when it happened, only twenty feet or so away from the barn door."

"And you had a plain view of the killer?"

"Yes."

"Will you point out the killer?"

"I certainly will." She gazed down our row of three Clement brothers and without any hesitation picked out Richmond's younger brother as the killer.

Prosecutor Toy smirked at us. "No more questions."

The Senator nudged me and whispered, "Ask her if she's completely positive of her identification. Act like you're downcast and upset about it." He tapped me on the knee. "Quick now."

I did as he directed. I sat there shaking my head for a moment and then looked down at the table. "No more questions."

"The State rests," Toy said.

I let the Senator call our one witness to the stand. While he examined him I watched Mrs. Ryan.

"Your name?" the Senator asked.

"Arthur Clement."

"Where do you live and what do you do?"

"I live in Missouri County, one north of here, and I'm mostly a farmer, but sometimes I preach a little."

"Are you a married man?"

"I sure hope so, sir. I've got ten children."

Several jurors laughed. Mrs. Ryan jumped when they did. She whispered something to Toy.

"You're not the defendant in this case?" the Senator asked.

"Not me, sir. My brother over there, Richmond, he's the defendant. He lives next to where Mr. Ryan used to live."

"Point out Richmond for the jury." Arthur did and the Senator had Richmond stand.

"Does he look any different now than he did on the day he was supposed to have killed Mr. Ryan?"

"He ain't changed," Arthur said, grinning a little.

Prosecutor Toy was raging. "We know they changed him over in the jail, Judge Steinmetz. That one on the stand is lying. I know . . ."

Steinmetz shook his head, stopping Toy. "I've known Richmond Clement for close to forty years and this witness isn't Richmond Clement." He smiled gently at the now enraged Toy. "You want to dismiss this or do you want me to direct a verdict, Mr. Toy?"

We sat in the office the next day. The celebration had gone on too long the night before. Even the sheriff had joined us for one drink, which soon became five or six, at the downtown Moose.

"Tell me once more, slowly, how you did it?" I asked.

"Well I got to thinking about the story of the fifty Chinese," the Senator said. "A lawyer in San Francisco was defending a Chinaman accused of theft. On the day of the trial he brought fifty Chinese men into the courtroom and had them sit with him and his client. No one could identify the defendant, and so he got off. It's an old story."

"I'd never heard it," I admitted. "But you didn't change Richmond Clement at all."

"There I played on the suspicions of Prosecutor Toy. We made the chief deputy think we did. We even let him watch some of the early work. He saw Lester Shay take Richmond and his brothers into a room. In the room Lester performed some work on Richmond. He lightly trimmed his hair and used pins to put it up so it looked much shorter. Then, later, after the chief deputy had been sent on, Shay did severely cut Arthur's hair. Shay used bleach on Clement's eyebrows and then darkened them again when the chief deputy was gone. He thinned Arthur's eyebrows and used bleach on them. He put Arthur into elevator shoes. Most important, we made Clement smile all the time after that night and made Arthur frown. The chief deputy took what he knew to the prosecutor. I bragged to him that we were going to make Arthur look so much like Richmond no one would ever know. That was enough. Toys are devious people, Don, so the plot had to be devious. We made Arthur look like what they thought Richmond would be." He looked moodily out his window, not completely happy about the deception. "I'd not have helped if Toy had let the lie detector in." He shook his head. "It won't work again in my lifetime, and it wouldn't have worked this time if the sheriff and the prosecutor hadn't been angry with each other."

"It saved Richmond's goose."

"On Ryan's wife, I understand she took it all very badly," the Senator said slyly.

"I watched her while you were questioning Arthur. She wasn't happy."

"It got worse. The bailiff told me she smacked her nephew with her purse in the hall and said he was the one who'd told her which one Richmond was. Cussed him good and mean. All this didn't make the prosecutor any happier and may even have made him angry. I understand he's now wanting her to take a lie detector test, relative or not."

"How do you know that?"

"She called here for you, but got me. She'd like us to

represent her in any further difficulties. She sounded a little worried."

"What did you tell her?"

"I told her we'd represent her." He smiled. "And I advised her she need not take any lie detector test. After all, from what the prosecutor himself has pronounced, they aren't reliable evidence in this county."

.

ONE WILL TOO MANY

Mark Wilhelm was what has come to be known within the legal profession as an "office lawyer." He had little ability for the fiery displays that help make the personality of a good courtroom tactician. He considered his mind to be too calculating and orderly for feigned heat and loud oratory. He was fairly adept at intricacies, at detail work, and so he existed well on settling estates, on minor tax work, and on abstracting titles to real estate.

He had certain abilities, certain faults. Among the former was his rather distinguished looks when he was dressed in his fine, dark clothes. Those looks made it possible for him to hold closely the attention of a widow when one visited his office, making each female client think that he regarded her as a more-than-friend. And, if sometimes the taste in his mouth was sour, still it was a living.

His practice was centered in a large Midwestern town. He liked the town, but it grew cold there in the winter. Very cold. Mark Wilhelm hated cold. He liked to spend those cold months in Florida, but vacation this year had been delayed by lack of funds and other reasons.

The most important reason was with him now on long-distance telephone.

"We haven't seen you. You've owed us more than forty thousand for almost a year," said the smooth voice that brought remembrance of daiquiris and suntans and horses that ran fast, but not fast enough. "When can we expect to get it? I rather dislike making these calls and I don't intend to call *you* again."

Mark's hands were wet and slippery as he held the phone.

"You know very well that gambling debts aren't legally collectible," he said weakly.

"Maybe they aren't in your business, but I'd hate to think they weren't in mine," the voice said, small slivers of steel beginning to show.

"Are you threatening me?" Mark asked, trying to raise the temperature of his voice with small success.

"Of course," the voice said. "That's exactly what I'm doing."

Mark started to hang up the telephone and got it all of an inch from his ear when resolve faded and fear came on. "I've got to have some time to raise that kind of money."

"I'll give you thirty days. If you don't have it then, I believe I'll assume you're never going to have it and proceed accordingly. One of my associates will call thirty days from today. Have the money ready for him."

Mark hung up the phone carefully and sat at his oversize desk thinking. He did not dislike himself for his compulsion to gamble. When you spent your working days around an office trying to make old women happy so you could write their wills and settle their estates when they died, a man deserved some bright lights and excitement when vacationing in Florida.

But last year he'd really gone off the deep end. Forty thousand dollars—

The opportunity offered itself the very next day. Mrs. Belle Rivera, a widow with cold, clutching hands, who had more money than the rest of Mark's menage together, died. And the nice part was that he didn't even have to help her along, as he'd done once or twice with other clients. Not really murder them, of course. Just leave a bottle of sleeping pills close when they were in pain, or that one time when he'd stolen Mrs. Jaymon's heart medicine.

Mrs. Rivera, Mark remembered well, was an eccentric lady with no close relatives who had doted strongly on Mark. He, in turn, had held her hand and his breath and waxed eloquent for her for years. And she'd trusted him.

Mark's main fault was that he was dishonest. It was a compelling dishonesty that would seldom allow him to complete a transaction without getting something that was not his.

In Mrs. Rivera's estate the fee for settlement, he computed, would be almost enough to pay his gambling debt, but it would leave nothing for another trip to Florida. The weather was growing cold and he longed for the warmth of the southern sun. Besides, he wouldn't be able to draw against the attorney's fee for at least six months. The probate commissioner was very strict about that. Also he owed the bank a great deal of money, and they'd move in on the major part of the fee.

He sat in his office thinking for a long time. Finally the idea came.

First of all he called her bank and his, the one that he usually worked with, and asked to speak to John Sims.

"Mrs. Rivera died this morning," he said to Sims. "Terrible loss. I've her will here in my office. She named your bank as executor and myself as attorney. I trust that's satisfactory?"

Sims happily assured him that the bank would be most willing to work with him in the matter.

"I'll probate her will this afternoon," Mark told him. "There were two copies and I've retained both of them here in my office."

"That's unusual," Sims said.

"She trusted me implicitly," Mark said, putting a little

ice in his voice. "She felt her will would be safer in my office than at her home. As you may know, she had become increasingly deaf and her sight was poor, and she was afraid that her servants might try to pry into her affairs."

"I see," Sims said, his voice satisfied.

Mark hung up the phone with relief, that part accomplished. What he'd said was perfectly true. Mrs. Rivera had left both copies of her will in his office. Now to change that will. But first he would have to contact his old associate, Alvin Light.

Alvin would be perfect for the idea he had in mind.

He told his idiot office girl he'd be out the rest of the morning and left.

The office girl had been chosen for two reasons. She was ugly and made none of his old lady friends jealous. Secondly, she was stupid and never noticed any of Mark's mistakes.

He found Alvin in a third-class bar doing what he was best at since he'd been disbarred—drinking. Outside the bar, though, before he went in, he watched with interest as an ambulance pulled up and loaded an old bum who lay tattered and supine in the gutter. None of the other bums paid much attention.

Mark heard one ambulance attendant grumble to the other: "Dead. This cold weather really gets to them."

The scene caught at something in his mind, an addition to the original idea. He stood thinking for a moment, then went into the bar. Alvin was holding drunken court in the back of the bar, but he shooed the bums away when Mark appeared.

Before Alvin's downfall for bribing a member of a petit jury and getting caught at it, the two had sliced up many a client between them. And even though Alvin was now a vile-smelling alcoholic, intelligence still showed dimly in his eyes.

Mark got him away from the bar and into the car.

"How'd you like to make fifty thousand dollars?" he asked.

Alvin's red eyes flickered. "I'd like it. Not for me so much. I'm smart enough to know what I am. But I'd like it for my boy. He hates my guts, but he's still my son. He's in medical school now, in California. He's married with a couple of kids I've never seen. He hasn't got any money, and he's going to have to drop out of school and go to work when this year is over. Enough money would see him through; the rest should buy me enough whiskey to finish killing me."

He looked up at Mark sharply. "What have you got going, Mark? I have to admire you, you know. I was a crook because I thought it was smart. You're dishonest because you're completely amoral—everything revolves around you." He sighed. "You've been luckier than I—a long time being caught."

Mark ignored the comment and went to the point, "You used to do Mrs. Rivera's work, didn't you?"

Alvin nodded. "She was a client of mine before you came along with your phony charm."

"She died," Mark said softly. "What if there was a bequest for a hundred thousand dollars to you in her will?"

"You mean there is one?"

"Not yet," Mark said, smiling. "But I have all copies of the will in my office and no one has seen them but me."

"I get fifty?"

"Same way we always went. Fifty-fifty." It was easy to say it. But there would be no split.

"How about witnesses to the will?"

"I was one. The other was my office girl. I didn't pick her for her brains. She's so dumb she has trouble remembering her own name. Besides, I typed the will and all she ever saw was the last page."

Alvin eyed him shrewdly and nodded. "Fifty thousand dollars is more than I'll ever need. Why so much for me? I might have gone for less."

"We've always gotten along at the even split," Mark said smoothly.

Alvin smiled. "Don't try to cross me on this, Mark. I need that money for my boy."

The rest was easy.

All he had to do was carefully take the staples out of the will, align the paper and insert, at the bottom of a page, among Mrs. Rivera's long list of specific bequests, a hundred-thousand-dollar one to Alvin Light, for "his past services to me and his present necessity." He would have preferred leaving it to himself, but that would be illegal, since he had drawn up and witnessed the will.

Then he probated the will.

The next four weeks went very smoothly. Mark lost himself in the intricacies of Mrs. Rivera's various problems. Final state and federal returns, inheritance tax schedules, waivers, inventories—nice detail work of the type in which he excelled.

Because Mrs. Rivera had died with a great deal of money and no close relatives, none of her heirs questioned her bequests. There was plenty for all. John Sims, probate officer at the bank, raised an eyebrow at Mark when he read the bequest to Alvin Light, but Mark pretended not to notice.

And so on the beautiful, but now very cold twenty-ninth day after Mark's long-distance telephone call, Alvin, armed with a check properly signed by John Sims, cashed that check, while Mark waited outside around the corner. Alvin was gone for a long time, but Mark was patient, if nervous.

When it was done they went back to Mark's office with a satchel containing a hundred thousand dollars and Mark got out a bottle of very good Bourbon and poured two drinks. He said: "This is the kind of day to be in Florida. Cold!" He shivered. "Drink some of this to warm you."

Alvin eyed the whiskey and Mark dubiously. "Just the one," he said.

"Of course," Mark said, and then watched while the one became two and then ten and conversation moved from old stories to monosyllables.

Everything went as planned. Mark thought of the whole hundred thousand and warm climates. He rationalized by realizing that Alvin couldn't be trusted. Alvin was an alcoholic and vain and sooner or later an alcoholic would part with any secret. And fifty thousand saved is an enormous saving.

After Alvin was suitably besotted Mark put him in the car, first carefully removing the money in Alvin's battered briefcase. He put most of this in his safe to pay the emissary of the gamblers and for his own future use. A few bills he kept for further use during the night.

He took Alvin to an even worse neighborhood than the one he'd originally visited the old lawyer in—a neighborhood known for muggings and knifings and doctored whiskey—and, of course, dead bums in the alleys.

Once, on the way, Alvin's eyes opened a little and Mark heard him whisper: "Don't cross me—the will—" and some gibberish following that.

Mark smiled and stopped his car in a deserted place and poured more whiskey down the weak old throat. Then he drove on. It was very cold outside and a light snow was falling. The car's heater could barely compensate. It was the kind of night to be heading south.

He dumped the older man in a little-used alley. This was the difficult and dangerous part, but Mark had been over the neighborhood thoroughly, figuring his chances, knowing they were good. He poured water he'd brought from the office over Alvin's sodden body, watchfully listening to distant street noises, careful and alert.

Alvin did not move when the water cascaded down. The snow was falling in a near blizzard now and the weather was very cold. He dragged Alvin behind a group of garbage cans and boxes. Twice more, during the night, he came back with more water, but the second trip was unnecessary. Alvin was dead.

Of course, there would be a furor about the hundred thousand dollars, but not the kind that a murder brings. Mark rehearsed his lines in his mind: "I told him to leave it with me or put it in a bank, but he was drunk. After all, he's been taking care of himself for a long time."

The hundred thousand could easily have been stolen by one of the toughs in the neighborhood. Mark scattered a few bills he'd kept for that purpose underneath the body and in Alvin's pockets.

The man from the Miami gambler came at eleven the next day. Mark had purposely let his office girl, "Dumb Dora," have the morning off.

The man was a nervous little wreck with a tic under his right eye and the face of a fallen saint. Mark smiled and escorted him to the inner office.

"You've got the money?" the little man asked.

Mark nodded and opened the safe and began counting it out in neat piles, hurrying, wanting to get this part done quickly.

"Good man," the nervous one said. "They were sure you weren't going to be able to come up with it. I'll have to get to a phone and call a certain number very soon now."

Mark increased the speed of his counting.

The interruption came then. Mark's door opened.

John Sims, the bank probate officer, was there. He had one of the uniformed guards with him.

"Sorry to break in, but there wasn't anyone in the outer office." Sims nodded apologetically at the little gambler's emissary. "This is important. They found poor Alvin Light's body in an alley a little while ago. Poor man had frozen to death."

Mark nodded, maintaining his composure. "Drinking too damned much."

Sims looked down at the desk, seeing the neat piles of money, and his face became curious. "I'm carrying out instructions. Alvin left a will with me yesterday when he picked up the money. Named the bank executor and you as attorney. He had me copy down all of the numbers and mark the wrappers of money I gave him yesterday. He stated in the will that if he should die suddenly I should come to you for the money immediately, that you would have it."

Sims looked down at the desk again and his face went blank. "Why, that looks like some of it there! I recognize the wrappers. You weren't going to use it, were you?" He picked up the neat bundles and handed them to the guard. "Alvin left the money to his son."

The nervous little man with the lost eyes sidled out of the office, while Sims and the guard gathered the money from the desk and safe. Mark tried to say something, to think of something.

Nothing came. Nothing at all.

Not *that* day anyway.

THE CHICKEN PLAYER

Jamie pulled the dusty, black T-bird onto the shoulder of the road he'd been cruising and sat there waiting. The radio was off because on a still day he could hear a car from farther away than he could see it.

In that hour of cruising he'd checked the road carefully. It wasn't in top condition, but it was all right, better than many he'd played the game on, and it had the advantage of sparse traffic, perhaps too sparse. The only other car he'd seen during that hour of driving was an old Chevy, worn out, down at the springs, driven by a man with white hair. Not very good prey, but a possible. The old man had driven by without a glance, moving very slowly. Jamie was still debating with himself whether to follow when he'd seen a child's curious face appear in the rear window of the old car.

That had ruined it. He was superstitious about kids, and there'd been enough bad luck recently. Thursday, he'd almost been arrested by a State Trooper, but had managed to outrun him. Friday, the transmission had gone out of the T-bird, and he'd been dismounted the whole weekend. Now, deep inside, he felt he'd about worn out this part of the country and it was time to move on. People were starting to look familiar to him, remind him of people he'd known before in other places and at other times. It was kooky how so many faces reminded him of Mr. Kelly. Mr. Kelly was thousands of miles away, back in New York State. Mr. Kelly was five years before in time.

Jamie remembered with narcissistic nostalgia that he'd been an amateur then, just learning the game. Then it had been a game of half-grown kids, played on deserted roads, with sentries out to warn if police came near. The Chicken Game. God, it had grabbed him even then.

The run at Mr. Kelly's car had been a lark, an impulse, a broadening of the game to include the world around Jamie. He'd have gotten away if he hadn't blown a tire at the critical moment. That had thrown him into the Kelly car when he thought himself safely past, and it had jumbled his hopped-up Ford into a junk pile, but he'd scrambled out unhurt.

He would not have thought that a kid could scream as much or as long as the Kelly boy had. Mr. Kelly had been thrown clear and he was unconscious, so only Jamie had to listen to the screams from the burning Kelly car. He had listened and felt strange inside, and when the screams stopped he'd giggled a little.

After a while there'd been lots of police and questions. "I lost control," he told them. "The tire blew and I lost control." He repeated it and repeated it and stubbornness and the good lawyer his aunt hired made the difference. The jury turned him loose.

Only Mr. Kelly knew. Jamie remembered the eyes that had burned right through him during the trial.

When it was done and Jamie was free he moved on. It was an act of protection, not fear. By that time he'd played again and again, and without the game there was nothing. No angry, vengeful man was going to take the game away.

So now he was twenty-three years old and he'd been playing the game for a long time. It was now a professional thing, done carefully, accomplished at rare, safe intervals when the desire became overpowering. The game was more than anything else, more than the sum total of all the rest. It was more than love, greater than sex, better than drugs, and stronger than the fear of death.

Sometimes when Jamie was around other people who were his age he could have screamed. The talk was mundane, the pleasures crude, and there was an eternal sameness to each scene. Sometimes he was sure that the only time he was really alive was when he was behind the wheel of the T-bird, alone, hunting. The rest of it was just the scene, all papery and fragile.

The game was simple, but there were rules. The other car was the mark. You passed it and accelerated away, making sure the highway was clear. A mile or so ahead you turned and came back at the mark, twisting right lane to left lane until the mark saw you. Then you took his lane, going straight for him, foot deep in the accelerator, forcing the mark to turn away, to chicken.

The rest of the game was of his own variation. When the mark turned away, Jamie followed, while the brutal, delicious fear rose within him.

Sometimes other drivers froze and stopped dead in the road and that filled Jamie with contempt. More often they came on erratically until he forced them from the road. Two months back he'd run a lone, male driver down a steep hill and seen him roll, metal shrieking, against rocks and trees until all sound stopped. That had been a very good one.

The game took nerve and a sure knowledge of the condition of the highway and an instinctive feel for what a car would do, but the shuddery exultation was worth all of it.

He'd not played the game for two weeks now and the last time had been a washout. He leaned back in the T-bird's bucket seat and thought and let the heat of anticipation wash over him. Vaguely he remembered his mother and father. They'd died when he was ten years old. It had been an accident on the Turnpike. A truck had smashed their car to nothingness. In a way, he was a child of speed. The insurance had made him near rich and he lived frugally now, except for cars. An indulgent, adoring aunt had raised him, given him his first car, protected him first from angry neighbors and later, the police.

A sound brought him back to awareness. He heard a far away motor and then he saw the tiny, fast moving car in his rearview mirror. He started the T-bird and listened to the sweet motor, the best that money could buy. He fastened his seat belt. Once he would have snarled at the idea of wearing a seat belt, but now the game was so precious that he took no chances and the belt held him firmly as he twisted back and forth.

He waited the other car out and it came past, moving fast—on the borderline of speeding. He caught a furtive glimpse of a lone, male driver who sat stiffly upright, appearing to be almost drawn back against the seat.

He gunned the T-bird out behind and passed the other car and was elated when it speeded up as he went around it. He could almost envision the other driver cursing him as he cut in sharply and pressed the accelerator down. There was no riding passenger in the other car. There was only the driver.

A perfect mark. *Oh Heat that lives within me: Make this one of the good ones.*

Jamie made his turn when the distance was right. There was no car behind the mark and nothing in his own rearview mirror. The heat began to build.

He let the engine wind up until the speedometer read ninety and he eased, right lane, then left lane.

He saw dust puff from the rear tires of the other car and something inside him screamed: *No! Don't quit on me!* The other car came on and Jamie smiled.

At three hundred feet away he slid the T-bird into the left lane, dead at the other car, anticipating what would happen. The other driver would panic now, move out of the path of Jamie's hurtling car. Then the variation. Jamie would follow, forcing the other driver away from the traveled road, onto the tricky shoulder.

At this moment Jamie liked to see the oncoming driver's face. He lifted his eyes and the face he saw seemed vaguely familiar and smiling, but that was impossible. Savagely, with hate, Jamie floorboarded the T-bird.

At fifty feet the other car cut sharply left and Jamie corrected happily, for this was as anticipated, but then the other car cut right again and there was no time to recover. The T-bird was caught slightly broadside. Jamie heard the thunder of the crash and fought the wheel and got the T-bird straightened as his wheels bounced on the shoulder, but one of the wheels hit a rut and he felt the T-bird going. He bent desperately into the seat, felt the top hit on the parched ground, heard the renewed tearing of metal and then it was a roll that seemed endless. The door came away beside him, but the belt held him firmly until all of the crazy, loud motion stopped and there was silence. Jamie reached then very quickly for the ignition, smelling the gasoline smell, breathing as hard as if he'd run a mile.

He could see the other car out of his starred windshield. Its right front end was smashed. The driver had the door open and he was unhooking a complicated safety harness that ran from a roll bar in the car over his shoulders and waist. It was the harness that had given him the stiff look, Jamie calculated.

Jamie unhooked his own seat belt, but the steering wheel was still in the way and his left leg was caught somewhere. He felt the beginning of pain, and the warmth of blood running down his injured leg brought a leaping panic.

"Help," he called.

The other man came slowly up to the jumbled T-bird.

"Hello, Jamie."

"I remember you," Jamie said incredulously. "You're Mr. Kelly."

"Can you make it out?" Mr. Kelly asked.

Jamie shook his head. "It's my leg."

Mr. Kelly's eyes sparkled.

Jamie looked at the other man, unable to read him, fighting away fear. "You like the game?"

Mr. Kelly smiled. "Enough to learn to play it. I trained in sports cars and drove dirt track for a while after my boy died and before I came after you."

"Maybe . . ."

Mr. Kelly held up his hand. "If they put you away you'd be back." He nodded. "There isn't any way to break you, Jamie."

"We could play again," Jamie said. "I've never had anyone before who could really play." He searched within. "It was better than it's ever been." And it had been.

"Not ever again, Jamie," Mr. Kelly said gently.

The fear came up in waves. "If you do anything, they'll find out somehow. You prosecuted me once. They'll catch you."

"Not about us," Mr. Kelly said. "You've changed your name too many times.

Jamie laughed, and the fear went away and he was exultant with triumph. "My fingerprints haven't changed. They took them then. They'll take them again. They'll use them and find out."

Mr. Kelly smiled a curious smile and sniffed at the gasoline fumes.

"I thought about that, too."

He lit a match.

When the screaming was all over, Mr. Kelly giggled.

THE CURLY CALLER

The voice on the phone was both muffled and menacing. "I hear you've got your first baby, Curly. Maybe soon, some night when you're out poking your nose where it oughtn't be, some night after your wife and baby come home from the hospital, I'll be calling on them."

"Where'd you make up the 'Curly' nickname from?" Bentz asked. At thirty years old his hair was as straight as the morals of an eighty-year-old virgin.

"That describes you," the caller said. "You're a man with a lot of curls. You bend my friends around in your courts. You hurt things. So you're Curly."

Bentz glanced over at the bedside clock. He was too sleepy to be really afraid. It was three o'clock in the morning. It had been about that time when his unknown, threatening caller had made the first call two days back.

"Take care, Curly," the voice said, and hung up. Both calls had been short and vicious. Bentz listened to the buzz of the phone for a moment before hanging up also. His home phone number, since he'd been prosecutor, was unlisted, but not unknown. The anonymous caller who referred to him as "Curly" was his first unknown caller of the night, but not his first caller. He'd had three calls from the police plus one call from an irate citizen (who'd been furnished the number by the police) complaining about a juvenile party going on next door, two calls from attorneys, and one call from a friend. Somehow, since he'd won election as prosecutor slightly more than three years back all callers expected him to be awake and alert at any hour. His record for calls was an even dozen between midnight and five o'clock in the morning, but he'd had a number of nights where that total had been approached.

Tomorrow Kate would be home from the hospital with the baby, a Kate who'd not wanted him to run for prosecutor before and who opposed his running for reelection.

Bentz tried to get back to sleep, worrying about Kate, worrying about the call, worrying about a dozen other things. Eventually, because he was very tired, he did sleep.

Lieutenant Dickson said, "I'll make a bet it's one of our gamblers."

"No way to know for sure," Bentz answered. "The timing's right though."

"Don't let it get to you," Dickson advised. "The ones who call to threaten you seldom bother you. This one is getting his kicks out of imagining you in fear." He smiled encouragingly. Bentz thought him a very good policeman, and they were close. Dickson had been after Bentz to run again, but Bentz, in the face of Kate's opposition, had been non-committal.

"This one says he'll stop by when I'm not at home."

"It's my opinion he won't, but I'll have them patrol the area near your house more often if you'd like."

Bentz nodded gratefully. "I pick up Kate and the baby today. When this guy calls it's going to frighten Kate." Bentz felt the anger of frustration rise in him.

"Why should it?" Dickson asked craftily. "Just answer as if it were a regular, business call. You're always telling me about how many you get at night. So say yes and no and not much else. Maybe he'll give it up." He nodded to himself and inspected the jackdaw grouping of official papers on his cluttered desk. "In the meantime I'll ask around, particularly among my betting friends. Maybe someone will say something to the wrong person. And again, my bet's on a gambler who doesn't want you to run."

Bentz nodded. Dickson knew most of the gamblers in the city of seventy thousand.

"And write down the time and date of each of those first two calls and also the time and date of any more you might get in the future," Dickson ordered. "It could come in handy." He nodded to himself. "You ever heard of reverse polarization?"

Bentz looked down at his watch. "No and I'm overdue in court."

"Another librarian?"

Bentz nodded. Off and on, over the past year, he'd been trying and plea bargaining a group of big money gamblers in the area. Dickson liked to refer to them as "librarians" because they were "bookies."

"Catch you later on it," Dickson said.

Bentz shuffled reverse polarization and the caller into the back of his mind for a few days. He picked up Kate and the baby and brought them home. There he worshipped them. Tiny Judith had days and nights mixed up. She slept contentedly between day feedings, but stayed angrily awake most nights. Bentz stoically learned about burping and diapers. Every time he tried to say anything about running again to Kate she looked stubborn. She was black Irish to his blond Dutch. She won most of the arguments he didn't have in court.

The next call came three nights later.

"You home?" the same muffled voice complained. "I called to talk with your wife about the new baby, Curly."

Bentz remembered what Lieutenant Dickson had advised.

"That won't be possible," he answered cautiously.

"Some night soon I expect it to be."

"See me tomorrow. I'll be in my office in the morning."

"I see. Yes, I understand," the caller said. "You're not letting her know what's going on. That's clever of you, Curly." The voice seemed suddenly louder, less muffled, as if whatever guarded the mouthpiece had slipped. Bentz thought the voice vaguely familiar, but then wondered if he was fooling himself. He heard thousands of voices a year.

Beside Bentz, in the big bed, Kate moved restlessly. Judith gave a whimper from her crib. Bentz dreaded the idea of both of them coming awake.

"What's your problem?" he asked softly.

"You're my problem, Curly. I want you bad. You've hurt a lot of my friends."

"Gambling friends?" Bentz asked.

There was a tiny silence. Then the voice continued. "Some night I'll get you, but before you there's your family. Your police watching won't stop me. I'll come calling. Till then, I'll keep watch."

Bentz felt a chill. Occasionally he did have to go out and leave Kate at nights. He'd have to continue if he stayed on as prosecutor. He had no control over what the time might be when he'd be called to the scene of a serious crime. He went when it seemed necessary. A determined watcher could bide his time, lie in wait, even with the police patrolling.

"Pleasant dreams, Curly," the caller said.

"Reverse polarization," Lieutenant Dickson explained, "is a method that allows a call to be traced back to the source even after his phone is rehung. I mean you tell me that he never talks long so we couldn't trace the call, but maybe this way might."

Bentz looked skeptical.

"It works, kind of," Dickson said. "We attach it to your phone. When your caller hangs up his line doesn't go dead and can still be traced back. Is it okay if I get some telephone people and try it?"

Bentz nodded.

"Don't expect a lot," Dickson said darkly. "We used it a few years ago around here on that half-baked high school extortionist case. There was a lot of stuff in the papers locally about it. I'd make a bet your smart caller knows about it. He's probably a careful man. But it's worth a try."

At an even dozen calls Bentz and Dickson had the device removed. The caller was using pay phones, a different one each time, usually one in a parking lot or along some night deserted street. And Kate kept wanting to know what the thing was that had been attached to their phone line.

"Keep up your log," Dickson advised doggedly.

Bentz was losing weight. He refused to announce a decision when party officials asked him about his candidacy. Rumors he'd not run got back to him. There was even a story circulating that the gamblers were laying two to one he'd not run. He ignored all rumors.

The calls continued sporadically into early spring. They were curiously irregular. Once a full ten days passed without one and Bentz searched the obituaries hopefully for a likely name. Once the caller missed a five-day period, but then called twice a day to make up.

Bentz lived a charmed life with Kate. She was so used to the night calls that she seldom asked questions. Once, when Bentz had to go out for a late night fatal accident, he had the police patrol closely and took his phone off the hook.

Bentz had forgotten about the mail. It arrived in the mornings after he'd left for work so there was nothing he could have done.

The night caller expanded his operations and wrote Kate a letter three days before the time for Bentz to file for office expired.

"Tell Curly not to file," the letter read in block print.

"Then he won't have to worry about his family health plan." No signature.

"It's from an anonymous caller who's been calling some," Bentz explained. The dam broke and he spilled a lot of it out. "Trying to scare me, scare you."

"How long's he been calling?"

"For a while. We're working hard to find out who it is."

"Is he why those telephone men were in here?"

Bentz nodded solemnly.

"He tries coming around here to hurt our little Judith and I'll take a butcher knife to him." She gave Bentz a fierce, loving look. "How many people hate you badly enough for doing your job to write like this, to call you?"

"Lots of dirty little people," he said.

"I want you to go make a list of them. Write all of them down who aren't in prison."

"What good would that do?" Bentz asked reasonably.

"I just want to know their names so that I can watch for them when you have to be out of the house running for prosecutor."

Bentz nodded and hugged her. He felt better than he had in months. The letter had backfired and aroused her competitive instincts. It was all right for her to tell him not to run, but not all right for anyone else.

To satisfy her he made up a list of about thirty names. He knew there were a lot more people than that who hated him, but he confined the list mostly to the gambling group because of his almost certain feeling it must be one of them. He'd been fairly successful in prosecuting them and had already sent some of them away.

As an afterthought he gave a copy of the list to Lieutenant Dickson.

"He's writing us letters now," he explained.

"That's federal," Dickson said.

"Okay. Remember the last time we tried to turn something over to them? It took months of paperwork."

"Turn the letter over anyway," Dickson encouraged.

"It's another avenue opened, someone else checking. You got the letter with you?"

Bentz gave it to him. "I didn't figure there'd be any fingerprints after you didn't find any in the phone booths."

Dickson read the letter. "You going to file?"

Bentz nodded and grinned. "Kate ordered me to do it today."

Dickson grinned too. "You filing ought to really set him off. You got that list of times you've been called?"

Bentz gave it to him.

"Those two times he missed for substantial periods intrigue me. A lot of people you or your deputies run through city court get five- and ten-day sentences."

Three days later Dickson had tentatively narrowed the list down to five names by checking both in and out jail situations. In the meantime, after the news stories on Bentz's filing appeared, there'd been a rash of phone calls, sometimes several a night, plus two more letters full of menace. Kate was now coming awake every time the phone rang at night. Even the baby seemed aware somehow of the tension. Bentz was still losing weight. Old Judge Stoddard, who seldom noticed anything, told him he needed a vacation.

"I've got to get some relief. You think you could talk your friends at the phone company into changing my number again?" Bentz asked Dickson.

"That would be very temporary," Dickson said. "Maybe better that I roust our five friends. All of them are petty people, tiny cogs in the gambling ring, too small time to get badly caught, but people who made enough money off the operation to resent you stopping it." He nodded. "All five of them fit the time script. They were out of jail when you got the calls and in jail or out of state when you didn't."

Bentz shook his head. If Dickson went beyond the law

and he let it happen, then it seemed to him he was no better than his adversaries. But there had to be a way.

An idea came.

"Dig around and get me telephone numbers where I'd have a good chance of catching each of the five at say two o'clock in the morning."

"Pay them back?"

"Not exactly. I only want to call them."

Dickson nodded. Next morning he presented Bentz with a list of four numbers.

"One of those guys kind of sleeps in the streets," he explained.

"Four's enough," Bentz said. *A chance.*

At just after two the following morning Bentz made four telephone calls, each call short and to the point. He then, after a good sleep, met Dickson, who seemed puzzled.

"So you called them? Accused them maybe?"

Bentz shook his head. "I need now to get around very quickly to where each of the four can see me."

Dickson nodded. "Two will be easies. They used to run bets and numbers from the courthouse wall. This kind of fine weather they'll be there."

They drove to the stone and brick building and parked in front. Bentz got out and walked past the pair after Dickson had pointed them out. They ignored him.

"Let's try the others," Bentz said.

They caught the next one coming out of a tiny store he owned a part interest in. Bentz got out of Dickson's unmarked car and walked toward him.

The man saw Bentz. He was a tiny man Bentz remembered sending off once for receiving stolen property, a man named Gartner. The little man gave him one agitated look and swiftly crossed the street.

Bentz grinned and went to Dickson's car and got in.

"That's my caller," he said.

"You want me to pick him up?" Dickson asked.

"No. I don't have a solid thing to hold him on and, in a way, he did me a favor. Without him and his calls and letters I don't think I'd be running again for prosecutor. But watch him. The thing about dealing with people like him is you see them lots of times."

"Okay. But please tell me how you figure he's the one?"

Bentz smiled. "Last night I made four calls. I told each person I called that my name was Curly and he'd better cross the street next time he saw me coming. Mr. Gartner there just did."

Gartner continued to cross the street during all of Bentz's second four-year term.

And the calls and letters stopped.

KILLER SCENT

The small man came into my courthouse office in the afternoon just after yet another report of *someone* spotting Joe Ringer. The man waited patiently while I ordered a car dispatched to the sighting area.

"Could I speak with you privately, Sheriff?" he then asked politely.

I examined him. He was so thin that he could be called emaciated. I thought him to be about my age, early forties. His handshake was soft and so somehow reserved. He wore rumpled, conservative clothes, thick glasses, and sported a small beard. He looked all right, but my sensitive nose smelled desperation and death, and I was distrustful of him. Most men trust something. I trust my nose.

"Edward Allen Reynolds," he said, introducing himself.

I nodded shortly. My long dead father once told me never to believe well of anyone who used three names.

"Sheriff Spain," I replied. "Things are busy. If you came to talk to Joe Ringer I'm sorry to report he somehow walked away from my jail last night."

He looked stricken. "I'd like to have talked to him, but not for what you probably think. My only interest is how he got to your town, Sheriff." He gave me a sharp look. "How'd he manage to just walk away?"

"If I knew, I'd be a happier man," I said, still not sure of his intentions. I'd thought at first he might be another reporter like the many who'd appeared in Crossville like wolves drawn to bait when we'd picked up Joe Ringer.

"If you aren't a reporter then what are you?" I asked.

"I'm a psychology professor at a small college in the East, but I'm on Sabbatical just now. If you'd like to check on me, you can call the head of the psychology department at your state university. He'll tell you I'm bona fide."

I considered doing that for a moment and decided against it. "I'm very busy," I said pointedly. "This is an election year." I tried to read his eyes behind their thick glasses, but nothing solid happened. There was only the faint smell to him of hurt or injury or desperation. "If you want to talk more about Joe Ringer I can recommend my deputy, Chick Gaitlin. He spotted Ringer in the bus station and arrested him." Gaitlin had been very popular with the disappointed newsmen all day.

"I think it's you I need to talk with, Sheriff," he said, lowering his voice. "I've got a theory that Joe Ringer was lured to your town for some reason I don't understand."

I smiled a little at that. "I've got an election opponent who's screaming all over the county today about my inefficiency, and I've got an escaped multiple murderer. I don't need wild theories. I do need to find Joe Ringer. Take your theories to the press. Perhaps they'd like them. They've turned Ringer into a folk hero instead of a cold killer."

"Please let me have a few moments of your time in private," he said. He looked around. The gum chewing deputy who was operating the radio was listening curiously. I'd heard he was the one who'd leaked things to my opponent all through the campaign. He'd probably been promised more rank and a better job after I was voted out. I knew he disliked me because I'd put him on the radio. Maybe he was the leak, maybe not. Election years make for chronic paranoia. I'd spent a lot of time getting where I was. I didn't plan to lose it. I had no wife, no family. I had only the job and the opportunities it brought.

"All right. Come into my private parlor, Edward Allen Reynolds," I said. I got up from the littered desk and led him into my dingy private office, closing the door behind us.

"First off I need to know how Joe Ringer got here?" he asked.

"Routinely enough. On a bus. A deputy saw him get off a bus and picked him up at the station. That was yesterday morning."

"But why would Ringer appear here? Why to this town, of all places?"

"Why not? Crossville's a nice town. Thirty thousand plus and growing. Industry, power, and farming. Read our Chamber of Commerce handouts."

"A lot of trails I've followed may have ended in your Crossville in the past few years, Sheriff. Did you ever hear of one Peter Green?"

"No," I said. I had, but I wanted Reynolds to talk, not me.

"I traced him here. He has a sister in Florida. I started there. He was a heavy suspect there and in some other states on maybe a dozen rape murders. She showed me his picture. Handsome young man who made his living as a long-distance trucker. Somehow young women died almost every time he was very long around a town. His sister told me he came to Crossville because of a very good job offer from some firm called Multiple Trucking

Incorporated. I checked them out earlier today. There isn't any company by that name around here and never has been. This sister hasn't heard from him since he left Florida. I've reason to suspect she never will again."

"I've sure never heard of the company," I said stolidly. "And I've lived all of my life around here. But so what?"

He shrugged. "Only that Green's missing in your town. I ran down one more certain, a construction worker named William Kole. I believe he killed for kicks, getting some kind of sick joy out of it, a butcher boy. He came out of Pennsylvania originally, but lived in San Francisco until he came here some months back. He was tried once in California for murder, but there wasn't enough evidence to make it stick. After the trial he moved here to work on your new power plant. I've got a copy of his work application. But when they tried to call him for work he'd disappeared. No one's seen him since." He shook his head, very intent, a man obsessed with his quest. "There have been some others I can't document as well yet. They apparently wound up here, but I can't prove it." He nodded positively. "I think they did. So I'll continue to check."

"All this is most interesting," I said, "but right now I'm a political candidate with a bad problem. I need to find Joe Ringer or start looking for a new job after the first of the year. And I like this job and also like to think I'm competent at it."

"I've heard around that you are, Sheriff. All I want is permission to stick close. I think Joe Ringer may have also been lured here. If I can talk with him then maybe I can find out exactly how."

"I don't need or want anyone in the way."

"A trade then. I've an idea or two about where Ringer might be found." He gave me a quick look. "All based on my research. I need to know something else first. Could he have been aided in his escape?"

"It's possible," I said, not liking to tell it. "He got away right at shift change time. He came out for a call after talking with his court-appointed attorney. Somehow he then just walked away."

"Who'd he call?"

I hesitated, not knowing how much to tell him. "We don't listen to prisoner phone calls."

"Come now, Sheriff Spain. Let's be truthful with each other. Ringer's a man suspected of at least thirty murders, men, women, children. He's a professional burglar and robber who enters homes and coldly kills anyone he finds inside, steals only the untraceables, and moves on. He's bright and careful and merciless. He's never been well caught. He's been tried twice and found innocent. I've got to think you cut a few corners on him. Who'd he call?"

I shook my head.

"What if I could name some names and one of them was who he called?"

"I'm not here to play games with you, Mr. Reynolds," I said, worried a little now.

"It's Professor Reynolds, really. Don't you want to find out what's happening in your town? What if Joe Ringer was lured here?"

"For what reason?" I asked.

"To be killed," he said.

"Then good riddance," I said, out of temper. "That won't bother me as long as it doesn't keep me from winning reelection."

"Nor me," he agreed softly. "But your problem is complicated because you've never found the bodies of any of the others, Sheriff. You won't find Ringer either unless you level with me. Please, let me give you my names."

I nodded reluctantly. He seemed sincere. But somehow I could still scent death on him.

He dug a piece of paper out of his pocket and began reading. I stopped him on the fourth name. Quinn Cowper. A farmer, a raiser of beef cattle. I knew him well.

"How'd you get your names?" I asked curiously.

"My list contains the names of everyone in your town that I ran onto in my little investigation. Cowper isn't the name I ran onto most. That one I won't share with you now. But apparently Cowper's the name we should be watching to catch Joe Ringer." He nodded at me. "Shall we go?"

I hesitated and then nodded. I led him out of the courthouse and past the old men who continually whittled their sticks on the wall. Some of them nodded at me, others did not. *Election year*.

Cowper lived north, down an old gravel road, miles from the interstate. I took Reynolds, but no one else.

We hid the marked car out of sight and walked up a hill. I carried my best high-powered rifle.

From the top of the hill you could see most of the Cowper place. There was a ramshackle old house, a fallen-in barn, and a few other out-of-repair outbuildings. There was a good fence tented at the top with barbed wire strands. We repair the fences first in my part of the country.

We sat in the dry, cool fall grass and watched. There was no immediate sign of life from the house, no movement, no smoke.

"I'll bet your man is there," Reynolds whispered beside me.

"Maybe, maybe not. I don't know why he would be there, and I still don't completely understand your interest. Why are you here?"

He gave me a strange look. "I need to know how it works. How does Cowper get multiple murderers to come here, perhaps die here? How does he know or recognize them, contact them, entice them?"

I sniffed the air. Soon the cold days would come.

"Why do you care?"

He gave me a peculiar look, and I knew I wasn't getting it all. "I'm a psychologist. All my life I've had some minor interest in the criminal mind. In the last few years that interest has been forcibly turned to mass murderers and multiple killers as a class. There seem suddenly to be more of them, as if because more people are being born, there needs to be a doubling or tripling of their ratio among us. I've got some figures . . ."

"Forcibly turned?" I asked, stopping him.

He held up a paper-thin hand. "Someone's come onto the porch down there. See?"

I looked at the farmhouse. There was someone.

"Is that Joe Ringer?" he asked.

The man below moved into better light. It was Ringer. I could see his pinched face and cold eyes. I nodded. "That's him."

He shook his head and whispered, "Not the one."

"That's Ringer," I said, perplexed. "Not which one?"

"Let's go down after him," Reynolds said, ignoring my question. He had a bad habit of doing that, and so puzzled me.

"Wait awhile," I said. "He looks as if he's waiting for someone. I'd like to know who." I wasn't ready to retake Ringer yet. I had too many questions unanswered about Reynolds.

"He's probably waiting for Cowper," Reynolds said.

"No, not Cowper," I said positively. "I know Cowper well, know he's in a hospital in a city forty miles from here. He was also there last night. I checked that out earlier." I smiled. "I thought maybe you might know who else it could be that Ringer's waiting for?"

He shook his head. "I truly don't. I swear it. We wait, then?"

"For a while. Someone helped him out, someone answered his call. I wish I knew who. What with civil rights, the Miranda case, and Supreme Court decisions on wiretaps, I can't let my deputies take chances on bending the rules these days."

"But maybe you took a chance?"

I shrugged noncommittally. I pointed downward through the red and yellow fall foliage, somehow wanting to move things along. "There's a cattle tunnel under the road. We'll go through it and get closer."

"Maybe we ought to do like you said and stay right here until we spot his helper," he said, hesitant now. "We've surely not been seen so far. He might see us if we start moving in on him."

"I'm running this show, Professor. I want to wait for your mystery man, but I've decided to do that waiting up close. So follow or stay here. Up to you."

He followed. We stayed behind trees and bushes and moved carefully. In a while we were within fifty yards of the house in a copse of trees. Joe Ringer, in the meantime, had disappeared back inside the house, but I could see movement now and then when he came to the front window and watched the road.

Insects whined about us voraciously as we waited out the long afternoon. Cars intermittently passed on the gravel road that paralleled the front fence. Professor Reynolds stiffened in anticipation each time one approached, but always the cars continued onward.

When the sun was almost down I made Reynolds move even closer to the house. Still no one came. Joe Ringer, now more confident as the light dimmed, came back onto the porch and impatiently watched the road.

"I'm going to have to go ahead and take him," I whispered finally. "It's getting dark. He could get away from us into the night."

"I need to know who he's waiting for," Reynolds whispered back angrily. "Remember that I found him for you."

I shook my head. I leveled my rifle and got Ringer in its sights.

"Stop right there, Ringer."

"Sheriff?" he called.

"Don't move."

He did what I'd thought he'd do and moved. He threw himself to the left and pulled desperately at his waistband. I bounced one errant shot through a window and hit him squarely with two more.

"No," Reynolds called, stricken. "No! I needed him."

"So did I," I said softly, thinking about my coming election. I moved cautiously to the porch, Reynolds following. Ringer lay unmoving. I'd aimed for his head. I foot-turned him. Already he smelled dead. A small caliber pistol lay beside him. I wrapped it in a handkerchief.

"You might have taken him without killing him," Reynolds accused.

I shook my head. "Not without taking bad chances. And not with you along. You saw his reaction when I called out. He went for his gun. He tried to get away."

"Where'd he get a gun?"

"Maybe the house," I said. "Maybe he found it inside the house."

I searched the body while he watched. I found the familiar note with Cowper's number on it, directions crudely printed to the farmhouse.

Reynolds said despondently, "Whoever it was could have been waiting out there for full dark, Sheriff. You've scared him off for good now." He shook his head. "This won't stop me. I'm going to go on looking. Someone in your town somehow got Ringer to come here. Someone didn't want him caught. *Someone*." He watched me.

I knew he was adding too many numbers in his head, and so I aimed the rifle at him.

He nodded, sure now. "Your name was on my list also. Top of the list."

I shook my head. "I've never had to kill anyone other than one of them. Cowper's my cousin. I take care of this place sometimes for him. I'm not going to be able to take a chance on your running around, talking. I've slept good until now. I'm thinking you'll keep me awake nights, Professor. I don't hate you like I do them."

He gave me an unafraid smile.

"How do you do it? Tell me how you spot them. How do you get them here?"

I shook my head. "I don't know where it came from, but I've had a very sensitive sense of smell all my life. A gift. A gift of smell. People like Ringer and Peter Green and the several others planted out there in ailing cousin Cowper's fields have an odor I can smell." I nodded. "I smell them out, acrid and pungent. It hurts me inside when I smell them. I got it first when I was only a kid. I wanted to kill that first one who smelled so bad, but I didn't because I was only about eight years old. Then, when I was deputying for Frank Stickney, we caught one who'd killed five people, and he smelled just like that first one. All he got from the law was thirty days for vagrancy because we couldn't prove a thing on the murders, and he just laughed at us when we asked him questions about them. When he was released I got him and put him in deep here."

"You smell them?" he asked.

I nodded. "Now, every year I go on vacation, plus the job takes me places. There aren't any more around here, but last year I was in San Francisco and this year it's supposed to be New York. I tell the police in the cities that I've got a man supposed to be in their city. I ask where's a good place for someone hiding to hang around. Sometimes I just wander. And you're right. There seem to be more of them all the time." I smiled. "It's not hard to find someone who has the smell, sometimes more than one someone."

"And so you kill them?" he asked, somehow eager to hear about it.

"Not then. I find out what I can about my candidates. I do it carefully. Most of them are as wary as old foxes and also very bright. Sometimes, after I learn what I can about him or her, for there are females of the species, I can figure a way to get them here, a ruse, a subterfuge. Joe Ringer fancied himself a writer. I found him and sent him a letter offering to publish his stuff. I paid his way here. It was just bad luck my deputy saw him and arrested him in the bus depot. So I had to let him escape.

It was easy enough. I wrote him a note to meet me here and smuggled it to him. I intercepted his call."

"And Peter Green?"

"He came to manage my trucking company."

He nodded, apparently delighted. I leveled the gun reluctantly.

"Not yet, please. You need to hear a few more important things before you decide on killing me." His eyes sparkled behind their thick-glass shields. For the first time they seemed alive. "Your deputies saw me leave with you for one thing."

"You tragically got in the line of fire," I said. "That's one of the reasons I missed with one shot. A sheriff doesn't have to answer many questions, especially with Joe Ringer dead." I shook my head. "Somehow you knew he was here and you led me to him. You died. I'll make you a hero, Professor, if that's any consolation."

He nodded approval. "That might work, but I've been tracking multiple murderers for a while. Others, all over the country, know about me and my fixation. I've never been as open with any of them as I was with you, but I never suspected any of them as I did you. I don't think any one of them took me seriously. You can hope not, anyway. I'll hope so, too. But someone could get very serious if I wound up dead."

That was something to think on, and I pondered it.

He waited patiently.

"I'm sorry. I don't have a choice. If I can win my election then, with luck, I'll have another four years of hunting them. And somehow I have to hunt them. Maybe I'm different, maybe I'm their specific for dying. I hate them as they hate us." I nodded at him. "Sometimes I think they're mutants, the coming race for earth. I've thought on it lots. Maybe they came along to wipe us out, take our places, be the survivors of the cities, mercilessly preying on each other after we're gone." My voice trembled a little.

"Easy, Sheriff Spain," he said soothingly. "I told you I

got into multiple murderers forcibly. Three years ago a man got into my house when I was away. He killed my daughter first. She was ten years old, quite pretty, already a small woman. He did things to her after she was dead. He then beat and raped my wife and left her for dead. She did die, but not for a long, hideous time, not before she told us—me—what he looked like. When my family died I also mostly died." He smiled without any humor at all. "Out there in your field would you perhaps have a man with a white patch of hair on the right side of his head, six feet or so tall, early thirties, hawk featured?"

I shook my head. "No one like that. Not yet."

"I see," he said, disappointed.

I waited. I'd lowered the gun.

He asked, "Did you ever think how much more efficiently you could work this if you had someone who knew psychology, who could figure out ways to bring even the cleverest of them within reach? A trained person?"

I considered the possibilities. There were hundreds of them out there, maybe thousands, enough for a lifetime.

"You could help me live again," he said softly, deciding for me. "I tracked you down to be your assistant."

THE IRON COLLECTOR

Bandon would never have gone to the division reunion if Sam Goins hadn't pressured him. Bandon, in spite of (or perhaps because of) his injuries, had never become much of a professional veteran. He despised the several other

local handicapped veterans who hung around the local
V.F.W. and the Legion, drinking free, telling war stories.

The idea of going to a reunion made him feel appre-
hensive. The service and its aftermath was a life he'd put
behind him, and so he tried to beg off.

"You go, Sam," he said. "Go for both of us. Call me and
tell me about it when you get back. And say *hello* for
me."

"No. The plans are set. I'm going to load you and your
chair into my car. I'll drive both ways and we'll stay in
the same room. I know you can drive, but I'm making it
easy for you. Some of the old boys have contacted me.
They say you don't answer letters. They *want* you there.
It's been a while, Bandon."

Bandon thought some more about it. Old memories
came back, some good, some bad. The division had come
home long after he was back. A few from the old company had come then, hushedly, to see him in the various
hospitals he'd inhabited for years, but other than Sam,
he'd not really seen anyone, or wanted to see anyone. And
it wasn't as if they wouldn't let him off from night clerk-
ing at the motel. He had time coming. He'd been extra
careful not to miss work, to be a dependable employee.

"I just don't think I want to go," he said slowly.

"Sure you do. Those guys are your friends."

Bandon smiled. A few weren't. When he'd been
wounded Captain Abrams had probably already been
scheming up charges against him, ways to lose him.

"What's good fun for you and the rest may not be fun
for me anymore. I'm not supposed to drink much."

"I swear you'll have a good time. Old comrades, old
stories. And besides, who came after you when you and
Abrams were wounded?" Goins waited, very sure of himself. They were old friends, out of the same town, and
Bandon owed him. Goins had even helped him get the
motel job.

And so Bandon went.

Sam Goins wheeled him into the huge meeting room in the Chicago hotel.

"Do you want a drink?" he asked.

"A beer maybe." Bandon looked carefully around. There were groups of men talking to each other all over the room, lots of men. In corners of the room white-aproned bartenders dispensed drinks.

"I'll see what I can hustle up. Wait right here."

"I won't stray far," Bandon said, smiling. He'd grown accustomed to being bound to the wheelchair, and now the remembrances of days before that time were shadows.

He sat hunched in the chair, looking around a little, nodding now and then at someone he either knew or thought he knew. The reunion was for the whole division, but Bandon had no interest other than in his own company, a hundred or so out of thousands.

As he looked he saw Captain Abrams.

Abrams was dressed in a baggy, brown suit. In its lapel there was a tiny, metal medal replica. He had a patch over one eye. His face, which Bandon remembered had once been almost too pretty for a man, was now lumpy and scarred, built into slightly different lines by clever plastic surgeons. The single remaining eye seemed about the same. In 'Nam Abrams had owned insolent, demanding eyes, proper eyes for the fair-haired hero of the division. The eye that now remained was still insolent, but not in quite the same way. Wary now, maybe—or puzzled.

Bandon, faced with the inevitable he'd both dreaded and desired, rolled that way.

"Hello," he said. *And up yours,* he thought.

The eye flicked over him, only vaguely interested.

"For just a moment," Abrams said loftily in his best company commander tone, "I didn't recognize you. I'd heard you were paralyzed." He smiled without humor. "But you're thin, Sergeant Bandon, and your hair's all gone gray." He nodded. "I remember the last time I saw you was when I got this." He pointed at the patch and face.

"And I got this," Bandon said equably, moving a wheel on his chair. "And we didn't find that weapons cache for the Colonel and that correspondent who was around." He smiled, remembering that.

"Too bad, too bad." Abrams looked at Bandon with clinical interest. "I thought you were dead after the barrage and before the medics came. I was sure of it. If I hadn't have believed that, I might have done something more about things when I learned later they never did find any weapons there."

"A tribesman told me," Bandon said, smiling again.

"What tribesman?"

Bandon shrugged. "A long time ago now. I guess I've forgotten."

"Maybe," Abrams said. "Maybe not."

Bandon ignored the tenor of Abrams' voice, not caring. "I thought you were dead also, Captain. I couldn't hear you after the mortar shells landed. First time ever for that."

Abrams took one step back and stared down at him. Bandon smiled some more.

Sam Goins came back then. He handed a beer to Bandon and nodded coolly to Abrams.

"Hello, Abrams." He didn't hold out his hand. "A few years since we've seen you. Last I heard you were running for office. Are you still in politics?"

Abrams inspected Goins with his single, wary eye. "Not these days, Corporal. In the old days people used to believe me even when they didn't like what I said. That was before Bandon here got me this face." He looked around the packed room. "Someone sent me a plane ticket and a note I was to be here to get a special award."

"An award?"

Abrams shrugged. "I guess. I'm at liberty just now, so I came." He nodded at the two of them, somehow dismissing them. "There's Colonel Glass over there. He's up in lots of things. I need to see him." He turned his back and walked away.

"He never missed an award," Goins said. "He never did miss one in 'Nam—never."

Bandon sipped his beer.

Goins watched Abrams retreating back. "If he hadn't gotten it, he'd have managed to get us all killed in a heroic charge one dark night."

Bandon had another sip. "Or day," he added.

Goins smiled down at him. "I said you'd have a good time, and seeing Abrams is an interesting start. I've found us a couple of old pals. Mac and Harlan are sitting over there. Let's go sit with them and drink and hate Abrams?"

"Let's roll," Bandon said.

They rolled and Bandon closed his eyes. He remembered Smitty lying dead and bloated in the hot, morning sun. He opened his eyes and watched the crowd, allowing Goins to navigate him. Through an opening Bandon saw Captain Abrams again hoisting a drink at one of the bars. Colonel Glass was there also, but his back was to Abrams.

Harlan and Mac were from the old company. They lounged at a table grinning at Bandon.

Mac raised a drink in salute.

"Hi, Sarge," Harlan said. "Goins said he'd get you here this time."

"This time?"

"Yeah. There was one like this three years ago. Didn't he tell you about that time?"

Bandon shook his head. Three years ago he'd been in a hospital, but Goins had said nothing about any earlier reunion.

"Abrams was here for that one, too. He was a joy. He drank too much too early, was loud, laughed lots, and at all the wrong times. He tried to be one of us boys, and it got real comical." He nodded at Bandon. "I guess Goins for sure didn't want you to miss it this time."

Bandon felt a tiny, cold touch in his spine at the line where everything died. Goins had always been a planner. "Why would he want me not to miss it?"

Harlan smiled. "My guess would be because you were

the only one with Abrams when he got it and you got it. We all knew Abrams was after you. Some of us heard later you'd said something to Colonel Glass when Smitty died and that Glass had bit a yard wide piece out of Abrams. Then you and Abrams somehow got wounded in an area Charley mortared lots. Some of us had a hard time figuring that out. How did an old pro like you wind up there?"

Bandon said nothing, but the ice spot grew a little.

Harlan continued. "If Abrams didn't like someone, they didn't last long. He'd put them on the point, he'd take them on his famous night patrols. There was Smitty. Before him there was Ryan and Lawrence and some others."

Bandon remembered very well. Smitty had been his friend. Ryan and Lawrence had been good men, but Smitty had been his friend. Abrams used a savage, completely understandable method in determining who took on jobs with great risks. He assigned those who fell out of grace and kept assigning them until they were killed or wounded badly enough to get sent back. And he volunteered himself and his company for everything. A medal hunter. "Iron Collectors," they were called.

Smitty had died on an Abrams-led night patrol. Ryan and Lawrence had disappeared into the green of the jungle while on point. No one had ever seen either of them again.

"Want a drink?" Harlan asked.

Bandon considered it. The doctors in the last hospital had said not to drink much, and he'd been faithful, most times, to their advice. He'd not expected to live long at first. When the years had passed and he'd remained stable, he'd been surprised and grateful. A man in a wheelchair is still a man. Bandon despised the chair and was not overly fond of his restricted life, but death seemed still worse, most days, anyway.

"Why not," he answered softly.

He remembered the afternoon, but only a little of the night. He stayed with Sam Goins and Harlan and Mac, but there were other familiar faces found, other hands to shake. After a time he could no longer propel himself and had to rely completely on someone pushing the chair. He drank to remember, then drank to forget. He listened to old jokes and lies and stories. And always, even when voices were at their loudest, he could hear underlying whispers, *Smitty, Abrams, Bandon.*

It was almost noon when he awoke. Sam Goins snored nearby in the other hotel bed.

The wheelchair was beside Bandon's bed and he rolled over to it, then levered himself into position in it on strong arms. His movements brought Goins up to a sitting position to watch him.

"You do that pretty good," Goins said.

"Yes. An acquired knowledge."

"Well, move it along smartly," Goins called after him as he rolled to the bath. "There's a special lunch. You'll want to be there to see your pal Captain Abrams get his award."

Bandon spun the chair around. "What's going on, Sam?"

"Nothing," Goins said. "Nothing at all."

"What sort of award?"

Goins shrugged.

In the bathroom Bandon felt ill, but after a bath and shave he was better. He let a solicitous Goins pour him a healing drink from an emergency suitcase bottle, and that helped more.

They went to the luncheon and sat with Harlan and Mac. There were at least five hundred others in the meeting and banquet room. There was a raised podium for the officers. Abrams sat at one end of it. His face was puffy, his single, baleful eye red. He picked at the food on his plate and Bandon, engaged in doing the same, realized the man had a bad hangover. Once, Abrams looked up and saw Bandon watching him. He frowned and looked

away, his face angry. Bandon smiled up at him in-
nocently.

Abrams had said that hot day long ago: "You're
next, Sergeant. There's nothing you can do, and you'll
soon know it. You've been at this a long time and you're
good at it, but that will only make it easier."

"Yes, sir," Bandon had said, hating Abrams for Smitty
and the rest and now for himself. Later he'd remembered
the area that Charley, for reasons known only to Charley,
mortared every day, precisely at four o'clock in the afternoon. Getting Abrams there had been simple. He'd told
Abrams a friend reported there were arms cached there.
And Abrams, eyes sparkling, had dreamed of yet another
medal, had thought Bandon was trying to redeem himself, buy out of peril.

Now, on the platform, they called Abrams' name. Colonel Glass read a list of his medals, Cross and Silver Star
and on down, an impressive list. He then presented
Abrams with a metal plaque listing the medals. Abrams
thanked the Colonel and sat abruptly down, dropping the
plaque on the table in front of him.

Bandon looked over at Sam Goins. Sam was smiling.
He winked at Bandon.

When the luncheon was done Bandon watched Abrams
stalk from the room. The plaque must have been less than
Abrams thought it would be, Bandon decided. The whole
affair was puzzling, but Bandon felt cheered about it. He
accepted a drink from Goins, then had another. Harlan
commandeered three bottles of champagne from somewhere and the four of them retired to Harlan's room.

Abrams was still conspicuously absent at the final banquet that evening.

Colonel Glass ordered the lights low and read a list of
the dead. A high percentage were from Abrams' company.

Bandon listened. Vietnam would soon be another old
war, forgotten except in history books.

Tomorrow, they'd go home.

Bandon went back to the room when the banquet was done, refusing further drinks, further parties. He lay awake for a while, remembering it all, hating what he was, trying to make sense of it. Then he slept.

In the night he came awake to sounds and light. There were at least a dozen men in the room. Each of them held a lighted candle, and Bandon was afraid for a moment until he saw they all were smiling.

Sam Goins had a typed piece of paper. He read awkwardly from it: ". . . to the one who saved us—to Bandon who battled the real enemy and won all of us a victory . . ."

When that was done each of them stepped past his bed and solemnly deposited old medals on his covers. There were Silver Stars and Bronze Stars, Purple Hearts, and mounds of campaign medals.

"We know what you did," Harlan said softly. "Maybe you saved more than only the company. The Captain, he had flair, he was brave, he was handsome, and he was flawed. Maybe, without you, he'd have gone on to some high place, maybe this, maybe that. Now he's just another man." He took Bandon's hands and pulled him up to a sitting position on the bed. "We bought his air ticket and had the plaque specially made for him, Bandon. It's made out of iron, polished iron."

Bandon saw the cruelty and the justice of it.

Mac nodded. "We all chipped in."

Sam Goins raised a glass. "To the good men we lost and to one we kept."

"Sure," Bandon said, smiling at all of them and at the pile of medals.

RODNEY PARISH FOR HIRE
(written with Harlan Ellison)

There was going to be a sorry boy on Farrow Street, and
Rodney Parish knew who it would be. It would be Rodney Parish, and he could already feel his daddy's strap
across his fanny. He hurried on through the twilight.
Mumblingly, he darned the kids who had urged him to
join them, illicitly swimming in the condemned pond behind the Chesapeake Lumber Company. He darned and
double-darned them, because he had missed dinner, and
Daddy grew madder than anything when that happened;
Rodney Parish's daddy used his big wide barber's strap
pretty often, and Rodney hated that, hated the hurting. It
wasn't worth the swimming. No indeed not! In fact, he
didn't much like his daddy, when it came right down to
it.

It was as he crossed Euclid Avenue that he saw the accident. The big blue car came out of the side street without stopping, and roared into the yellow-and-gray car
with a smashing roar that made Rodney jump, and clutch
at his ears. Rodney stared through his thick lenses at the
two cars, and it made his strangely-pudgy face squish up
like when Miss Dexter made the chalk skip on the board.
He ran over and looked in the yellow-and-gray car. The
man was crushed up against the door, and the steering
wheel had been driven through his chest. The man was
not breathing, and Rodney noticed with interest that a
yellow tinge had come over the open eyes. A man with
gray hair and a plaid vest stumbled out of the blue car,
and staggered up to the broken window through which

Rodney stared at the dead man. Rodney wanted to giggle at the way he looked.

The man in the plaid vest put his fist in his mouth, like he wanted to eat it, and he started moaning like Noobie when the cat scratched at his ears. Then the man in the plaid vest came around the car, and sank down on his knees in front of Rodney.

He wasn't much taller, then.

"Listen, listen to me good, kid," the man said, and Rodney Parish noticed he was crying like a girl or something. "Listen, kid. If anyone, if anyone asks you what happened, tell 'em . . . tell 'em . . . this guy was coming real fast down the street and hit me after I'd stopped . . ."

He went on for a long time, explaining it really good for Rodney, so Rodney could blame it on the dead guy, and that wasn't right until the man in the plaid vest promised to give Rodney fifty dollars, and gave it to him, right there.

Then it was all right, and Rodney told the policeman what the man in the plaid vest had told him to say. That was okay, then.

Then it was worth getting strapped by Daddy.

Then it was okay, coming home late.

It took Rodney Parish only four months and thirteen days to realize how that sort of thing could be used. It was just renting yourself out, like Daddy did when he cut the men's hair downtown. It was okay doing that.

As long as you got what you wanted.

Because it felt good inside, doing bad like that.

Of course you couldn't always count on seeing an accident and having a nice man, like the man in the plaid vest, give you fifty dollars for a simple little thing like changing a story. But Rodney kept remembering the way the man in the car had looked, with the nice red stuff pouring out of his chest and the liquid, yellow look to the eyes. Besides, the fifty dollars hadn't done him much good, not dribbled out the way he'd had to do it. He'd been smart enough to know that he couldn't go out and

buy a bunch of new things, things that he wanted for his
stamp collection, for his coin collection, for his baseball
picture collection. New acquisitions brought questions, so
the fifty dollars had to be spaced out, but in four months
it was gone.

And there were still gaps in all of the collections.

Of all of the kids at the Twelfth Avenue school the one
Rodney hated most was Jimmie Larkin. He was the one
who'd started the hated nickname that Rodney now bore
on the playground—"Owl Eyes."

Jimmie was the first one to die.

Rodney did it for a tongue-tied little Italian boy named
Salvatore Maggini. His reward was an 1898 Indian Head
penny, which filled a vacant slot in his coin board. Of all
the kids that Jimmie Larkin picked on, Salvatore was his
prime target.

It was Salvatore that Jimmie beat up every day for a
solid week. It was Salvatore that Jimmie pummeled and
ridiculed at every recess.

At first Rodney "Owl Eyes" Parish was merely relieved
that it wasn't he that was getting the lumps from over-
muscled Jimmie. But then the idea that had begun some
four months ago in fertile ground sprung out its first
green leaflets. People who were the way the man in the
yellow-and-gray car had been couldn't pick on you. People who were in the shoes of the man in the blue car—
well, they would pay.

He caught Salvatore in the boys' rest room, where he
was spending a miserable recess hiding from Jimmie
Larkin.

"How'd ya like it if that old Jimmie Larkin never bothered you again."

The black eyes came up to his. "Go on," Salvatore managed to stutter, "you can't whip him."

"You gimme your Indian Head penny, and I'll make
sure he never bothers you again." Rodney scuffed one
shoe over the other. "By day after tomorrow."

There was hate and fear in Salvatore's eyes. But there was also hope. He nodded.

"Gimme now," Rodney said. He held out his hand.

Salvatore filled it.

Jimmie was easy. Despite his muscles he was dull witted.

Rodney sidled up to him after school.

"Hey Jimmie," he said.

Jimmie looked back at him with infinite disgust. "Whatcha want, Owl Eyes?"

Rodney smiled his most ingratiating smile. "I got something I want to give you if you'll walk home with me."

"What?"

"You know that old baseball glove I got, the one with the stuffing out? Well, you can have it." He shook his head. "I don't like baseball, anyway."

Tenth Avenue and Farrow Street was the busiest intersection in town. Jimmie Larkin died under a truck there. All it took was an outstretched foot as they raced across to beat traffic.

Jimmie looked even better than the man in the car who'd died. All smashed and gray and with his eyes starting out of his head.

In the next six months there were three others. Not all from the Twelfth Avenue school of course. The need for Rodney's particular talent was spread around. And all payment in advance.

There was the blond girl at the old pond behind the lumber company—the one who insisted on stomping the pigtailed girl's mud pies as quickly as she made them. The pigtailed girl had a stamp that Rodney coveted. He waited while the mud-pie girl ran home for the stamp. Then he drowned the blond girl after stunning her with a piece of wood. That one hadn't been particularly enjoyable as they'd made him leave and he never had seen the blond one's body. But it was summer work.

The best one was the boy at school he'd pushed out the

window. They'd washed for days and never got the pink tinge out of the sidewalk. Rodney made the place a shrine. He could get a thrill just standing near it.

He was the best because he was a tattletale, and three kids had all chipped in to get rid of him; they had each contributed ten baseball pictures. Rodney Parish's most important hobby of all. Thirty pictures, almost every player on the Dodgers and Yankees, with the exception of the real-hard-to-get Mickey Mantle card.

It was the Mickey Mantle card that eventually caused the death of Leroy Tarvish.

Owl Eyes stood in the shadow of the building, near the concrete apron with its six manholes down which they dumped coal for the school; the concrete apron on which the kids played "pussy-in-a-corner." He stood there with his odd pudgy face squished up, with his crewcut bothering him—the haircut had been the day before and little pieces of it were down his back itching worse than anything—and his soft, blue eyes behind their great lenses staring at the scene on the playground. His glasses were dirty, but he saw it all right.

Arville Hickerson was the rich boy, and he was all the time trying to make friends with Leroy Tarvish and his bunch of rough kids. Leroy all the time shoved Arville and told him:

"G'wan, you skinny piece'a dog-pee," and that made Arville madder and madder, until he would give *anything* to kill Leroy Tarvish.

Even his Mickey Mantle baseball card from the bubble gum. And that was hard to get, because they only packed maybe one of that kind of card in a box, and nobody else in the whole neighborhood had it but Arville Hickerson, and that was only because he had a rich old man.

So Rodney Parish made it known to Arville that he was available. For a price.

With the Mickey Mantle card safe inside the stack of pictures, the rubber band holding it snugly between

Johnny Logan and Roy McMillan, Rodney waited for his time. He had become an expert in his way. He was the smartest kid in the block, no matter *what* that snotty old Miss Dexter said!

The time came.

Leroy Tarvish had to wait for his older sister, Sophie, one afternoon. All the rest of his gang had gone home, and he was just sitting around the schoolyard, doing nothing very much, just waiting for his old sister to come on out so he could go home and watch TV for a while.

"Hey, Leroy!"

Leroy looked up from his game of mumbledy-peg and saw Owl Eyes coming across the schoolyard. Leroy didn't like Owl Eyes; he gave him the scrimmies, somehow. There was something real—whatchamacallit—queer about Owl Eyes. He was all the time collectin' something.

"Whatcha want, Owl Eyes?" he said the name nasty because he was sure it would bother Owl Eyes.

"Wanna play?"

"Play what? No, uh-uh, I don't wanna play nothin'. I'm waitin' for my sister, then I'm goin' home to watch the TV."

"Thought'ch'd like to play for a while before your sister comes out. Why'd she hafta stay after school?"

"None'a your business, Mr. Big Eyes."

"Bet she was bad!"

"You're stupid, too. She's beatin' erasers for Mrs. Hollowell, that's why, you stupid dope."

But after a while, he gave in, and they teeter-tottered for a few minutes, and ran around until Leroy tripped Rodney Parish and made his glasses all dirty. Then Rodney said, "Hey, get onna swing. I'll make you go high."

"Okay."

So Leroy Tarvish went high. Very high and very fast, and at just the right moment, at just the right speed, Rodney Parish slammed the swing sidewise, flinging Leroy Tarvish into the metal pole bracing the swing. Leroy

Tarvish's head hit with a crunch and stuff came out even after he lay there in the dirt.

And not till he had straightened up, after crouching for a long time watching the gray stuff, did Rodney Parish realize Leroy Tarvish's sister, Sophie, was standing by the school door, giggling.

Rodney grew tired quickly, perhaps because Sophie was older. But he did not catch her that afternoon. And the next day no one said anything to him about Leroy Tarvish, so he knew Sophie Tarvish had not ratted on him. But she was a stinker, and he knew she would have to die.

He thought he had her that afternoon, when he followed her into the girls' toilet, but Mrs. Kneipper saw him and dragged him out with indignation. He could have shoved Sophie out the window and she would have died beside the flag pole on the sidewalk.

It made Rodney feel high and warm and nice to think about it.

But she continued to elude him, and it wasn't until three days later that he saw her going down to the basement of the school. He followed her.

She went into the big room that said NO ADMITTANCE, where the coal bins were, under the manholes on the "pussy-in-a-corner" game. It was dark and scary in there, but he went in, too.

"Sophie? You in here?" he asked.

"I'm in here, you stinky you!" she answered.

"I'm gonna kill you like your old brother, just like him, and you'll bleed and be dead and rot and stink too, you're such a—"

There was such a rush of chill air that Rodney for a moment did not realize Sophie had crept up on him, and swatted the air in front of his face.

She was taunting him. She ran farther back into the bins.

"I'll get you, you old rat-stink you! I've killed lotsa

other kids and got paid for it, too, so that's how much *you* know! So you ain't so good!"

He was back in the bins, feeling the pieces of hard black coal under his shoes. The bins were almost empty. He'd catch her and smash her old head in.

There was a distant muttering from above. He looked up and all there was to see was the light-line made by the circle of the coal bin manhole cover. He stretched his hands out in front of him to find her, but it was so very dark.

Then, abruptly, Sophie was behind him, and she swatted at him again, calling him dirty names, and he was going to say, "Sticks and stones can break my bones—" but her hand knocked off his thick glasses, and he was stumbling around in the darkness, crying.

Then somebody pried off the manhole cover, and he heard the distant thunder that was the truck rolling up, and as Sophie ran back out through the door she yelled, "You old dope, you! I knew they'd be bringin' it today!"

And Rodney Parish stumbled around with the word *dope* in his head, crying to be let out, until they dumped three tons of hard, black anthracite on him.

Sophie stood by the swings and watched the truck roll away. Then she turned and started home. That stupid boy! If he hadn't kept bothering her, she wouldn't have had to do anything bad to him. She wasn't going to tattle; she didn't like Leroy Tarvish, her brother, very much, anyhow. He was always kicking her.

But that had been interesting, what Owl Eyes had said about killing kids and getting paid. A new two-wheeler, and the extra clothes for the Dolly Dimples she got for her birthday, and . . .

She wondered, as she hurried home, if she should have cards made up, like that cowboy on the TV.

DO-IT-YOURSELF
(written with Harlan Ellison)

Madge retina-printed her identity on the receipt, fished in her apron for a coin, and came up with a thirty-center. It was a bit too much to give the boy, but she already had it in her hand, and there *were* appearances to keep up. She handed it across, and took the carton.

A tremor of pleasure swept her as she was closing the door; the messenger boy was assaying her figure. It had been years, or longer than that, since a young man had done that. Perhaps it was the new rinse. She closed the door firmly and blanked it, patting her hair. Yes, it was the blond rinse, that was it.

Abruptly, she realized she had been standing there, staring at the box in her hands, for some time. With mild terror.

Madge Rubichek, she chided herself, *you contracted for this, and now it's here, and it's paid for, so what are you making faces like that for? Go in and sit down and open it, you silly goose!*

In the kitchen, she took a paring knife to the thick, white scotchseal of the carton. The box was secured around the edges, and she inserted the paring knife as she would have with a carton of soda crackers. She slit it open down one side, up the next.

Except this was not a carton of soda crackers.

Nor bran-soya flakes.

Nor baking sperm.

Nor cake mix.

This was—oh, how odd—a do-it-yourself kit. A modern

marvel like all the new do-it-yourself marvels. Do-it-yourself house-painting setups, and do-it-yourself baked-
Alaska mix, and do-it-yourself this and that and the other
thing. There were even advertisements for do-it-yourself
swamp-digging kits, for chassis-aligning kits and pruning
kits.

But this was a particularly odd kind of kit Madge had
purchased:

To be precise, a do-it-yourself murder kit.

Madge Rubichek busied herself lifting the top from the
carton. She set the box top beside her chair and pulled
away the tissue paper double-folded over the carton's
contents.

What odd-looking mechanisms. Even for 1977, which
Madge had always called—in the sanctum of her mind,
where profanity was permitted—"too damned machiney
for its own good!" these were strange.

There was a long, thin, coiled sticky-looking tube of
gray something-or-other with a valve at one end and a
blow-nozzle attached.

Beside the coil of gray tubing, hooked to it by soft wire
and wrapped in tissue paper like a Christmas necklace,
was another small parcel. She lifted it out, surprised at its
heaviness, and stripped away the tissue.

It was a small glass square, obviously a bottle of some
sort, filled with a murky, mercurial-seeming liquid that
moved rapidly as she turned the container, sending up no
air bubbles as it rolled in the bottle. It had a tiny, pin-like
protuberance at one corner, with a boot fastened down on
it, easily snapped off to open the vial. Quicksilver? She
found this item as mystifying as the preceding one. She
stared at it a moment longer, with no apparent function
coming to mind, and then she laid it aside.

The next was a layer in itself; rather thick and quite
black, it was almost of the consistency of an old beach
ball, or a fish skin without scales, or—

What?

She pulled it free, and almost immediately let it drop

into the leaning carton top beside her chair. She just didn't want to *touch* it. Mental images of dead babies and salamanders and polyethylene bags filled with vomit came to mind when her fingers touched that night-black stuff.

She dropped it free, and found beneath it a pamphlet without a title, and a small glass globe with all the attributes of a snowstorm paperweight, the kind her grandfather had had on his desk in the old law offices in Prestonsburg. It was on an onyx stand of some cheap material, and the globe itself swirled and frothed with the artificial whateveritwas inside. But there was no little town once the snow settled, and no large thoraxed snowman with anthracite eyes, and no church. There was nothing in there but the lacy swirlingness. The snow just continued to whirl about, no matter how long it lay in one position. It would not settle.

She put it beside her on the chair, and nudged the carton, now empty, off her lap. She took the pamphlet in her hands, and opened it to the first page.

"Hello," it said in a rich baritone. It was a comforting voice, and one that was subtly reassuring, as well as inviting attention and forthrightness of manner, clarity of thinking, boldness of approach.

It was a mellow and warm voice.

It was, apparently, the voice of murder.

"This is your own Do-It-Yourself Murder Kit," the pamphlet continued. "The *new*, guaranteed Murder Kit, with the double-your-money-back warranty, for your protection."

Well, she thought, frugally, *that's nice, anyway. That double-your-money-back thing*.

"This Kit contains three sure, clean and undetectable, I repeat, *undetectable*, ways to commit murder. Each of the three *modus operandi* is designed for you according to the application blank you sent us when you contracted for this Kit. Now. To prepare yourself for your murder—"

She snapped the pamphlet shut with quick, suddenly-sweating hands.

Do I hate him that much?

Where had their marriage gone wrong . . . somewhere in the eleven years? Where? An infinite sadness stole over her as she remembered Carl the way he had been when they first met. She remembered his ways, that had seemed rough and yet gentle, masculine yet graceful. And she recalled her own aristocratic nature, the fine background, and the womanly ways. But how had it changed?

She conjured up visions of it now. The ashes on the carpets and the smell of musty cigar smoke that stayed in the curtains and chair coverings no matter how much she aired and cleaned. She remembered the fat, nasty belly of the man while he sat pouring bock down his dribble-chinned throat, the clothes rank with sweat strewn across her immaculate bedroom, the rings in the bathtub, his rotten teeth . . .

And of course the quick animal urges all panting and grunting that were nothing but revulsion to her.

She answered her question firmly: *Yes; yes, I hate him that much!*

She opened the pamphlet again. Her hands had become dry and cool again.

"The first method of murder we have prepared for you," the pamphlet's voice continued, undaunted, "is the rabid dog method. You will notice a coil of gray substance. This is your Animaux Tube. Warning is issued at this point that instructions throughout the use of this Kit must be *specifically* followed, or failure will result. There is no mechanical failure possible with this Kit, only *human* failure through inefficiency and disregard of stated operating procedures. Is this understood?"

"Yes, I suppose so," Madge answered, surlily.

"With your Animaux Tube, attached by wire, is a vial of Essence, a specially-produced, copyrighted substance to be used *only* with the Animaux Tube. Again warning is issued to preclude any ill-use of materials included in your Kit. Unspecified use of the Essence included in your Kit will prove most unpleasant. In the human digestive tract it reacts violently, causing almost immediate convulsions and death. Care should be exercised to keep the vial away from children and pets."

She lifted the coil of stuff and it *was* sticky. After spreading a sheet of newsfax on the rug, she allowed the gray tubing to unroll itself out onto the fax sheet. There was no sense ruining a good rug with any odd chemicals from this Kit. She had always been a methodically neat woman, and just because she was doing what she was doing, was no reason to become a crude slob—like Carl.

"Take some article of clothing belonging to the intended victim," the pamphlet voice continued, startling her, "and place a small piece of it firmly against the Animaux Tube, on the orange blotch near its front. Press it, and it will adhere. Then inflate the Tube by blowing gently and evenly into the nozzle. Only after the Animaux Tube has been inflated should the Essence then be added. Screw the vial of Essence onto the air valve and allow it to drain completely into the Animaux Tube. Make certain that every drop enters. You will then have your Animaux rabid dog. Set the dog loose when the intended victim is near and it will inflict a bite wound that will cause violent death within a matter of minutes."

She used one of his socks, holding it as far away from her as possible. It was hideously pungent and ripe after only one wearing. The dog itself took shape quickly. The Tube seemed to retain the air blown into it; there was no blowback. The surge of anticipation turned her hands clumsily when she hooked the Essence to the blown-up Tube and a few drops spilled onto the newsfax underneath it.

The thing moved softly. It looked for all the world like a medium-sized mongrel dog of no apparent lineage.

It limped toward the door and stood there whining, its jaws slavering.

"Not for a few more minutes," she told it soothingly,

afraid of it herself, yet exhilarated by what she was doing, what was to be done soon enough. "He won't be getting off the slipway for a few minutes." She spent the time neatly hiding the rest of the Kit and the now-silent pamphlet in her clothes closet, at the bottom of a moth-proof garment safette. Then, when it was time, she let the dog out.

Carl came gruffily into the house, cursing foully, and her heart sank.

"Damn dog tried t'bite me when I got offa the express-walk. Thing musta been sick." He nodded proudly, "Kicked it an' the sonofabitch died right there. Real soggy mess," and he laughed. "Never even touched me."

The next morning, as soon as he had slipped to work, as soon as she had watched the slipway carry him out of sight over the horizon to the Bactericidal Dome, she took the Kit from its hiding place at the bottom of the moth-proof garment safette, and carried it into the dining nook. She was really annoyed; this Kit had cost a lot and she wanted value for her money.

She punched herself a second cup of coffee and opened the pamphlet again.

"If you failed," the booklet began, as though anticipating her anger, "it was, as I warned you, through human error, and not on the part of this Kit. Was your murder a success?"

"No!" she answered, in a pique.

The pamphlet was silent for an instant, as though refraining from taking offense. Then it began: "If you have not succeeded, attribute your failure to one of the following:

"One. You snagged your Animaux Tube and it was not fully inflated, or later lost air.

"Two. You did not allow the Essence to fill the Tube completely. Perhaps you spilled a portion.

"Three. You prepared your rabid dog for the scent improperly.

"Four. You did not attach your Essence vial properly, causing irreparable damage from leakage.

"Well, do one of these fit your case?"

The pamphlet waited, and she remembered the few drops of substance that had trickled free in her eagerness to set the dog loose on Carl. She mumbled something.

"What?" asked the pamphlet.

"I said, I spilled some!"

"Ah so," the pamphlet agreed. "Undoubtedly, certain vital organs were not properly formed, causing a malfunction of the pseudo-beast."

Recollections formed of the evening before, and she saw the rabid animal again, froth dripping from its viciously-spiked jaws . . . limping and whining. So *that* was it. Well, it wouldn't happen again.

"What do I do now?" she asked.

The pamphlet seemed to make a snickering sound, as if it were acknowledging her loss of annoyance at it, and her own recognized sense of failure, her inferiority. It might be said the pamphlet was its own brand of snob.

Then its snideness disappeared, and the booklet advised, "Remove the Deadly Nightshade from your Kit. Be careful *not* to spread it out. Repeat, do *not* unfold it!"

She knew at once what was meant. The black sheet with the horrible feeling of dead flesh.

She hesitated to touch it; nonetheless, she reached into the Kit and brought out the layer of softly-folded, unbelievably black, ghastly-feeling material. She dropped it at her feet.

"Are you ready?" asked the pamphlet.

"Yes, thank you."

"Excellent. Now this second method allows less room for human error.

"If you follow my instructions to the exact letter *precisely*—and I cannot stress this enough—you will have accomplished your desire by morning.

"Your Deadly Nightshade is a copyrighted, patented"—
it reeled off, in bored voice, a string of Guatemalan Pat-
ent Authority designates—"exclusive with the Do-It-Yourself Murder Kit." She realized at once that the voice was
huckstering out of necessity, that it found such commer-
cialism odious, vulgar and tedious.

"Place it in the bedroom of the one you wish to elimi-
nate. It is very important that this be done precisely as
directed. On no account should you, after placing the
Deadly Nightshade in the bedroom, reenter it before the
intended victim. The Deadly Nightshade acts as a controlled form of narcolepsy, by the release of hypnotically-
keyed visual and mental depressants. The intended victim
is cast into a hypnotic spell of long night. In three days he
or she will *sleep* all life away. The room will be a place of
perpetual darkness to him or her and slowly the vital bod-
ily functions will fail and cease.

"However, it is very important that you place the
Nightshade in the intended's room evenly and without
wrinkles, stretching it out under the bed or somewhere
else where it will escape observation. And . . . you must
not reenter the room once you have placed the Deadly
Nightshade. Exposure begins once the sheet is spread."

She shook it out like a chenille bedspread and laid it
out neatly, placing it very carefully under the bed, once
again laying out newsfax to avoid any later unpleasantness
to the floor. She tidied the bed, tucking in the blankets as
tight as those on the bunk of an army King/Sgt. She
spread the Deadly Nightshade in a tight, wrinkle-free
sheet.

She missed seeing the socks, somehow.

They were on the floor, just peeping out from under the
bed, half-under the Deadly Nightshade.

She caught them out of the corner of her eye, just as
she pulled the door to behind herself. Carl's filthy socks!

She remembered the instructions clearly.

"*. . . you must not reenter the room once you have*

*placed the Deadly Nightshade. Exposure begins once the
sheet is spread . . ."*

Well! She certainly wasn't going to chance *that*.

She got a broom from the broom-closet, then reopened
the door, and yes . . . just by holding the broom tightly
at the sucker-straws, by keeping her wrist flexed and tight
to maintain rigid balanced control, she was able to snag
the socks, one by one.

Madge congratulated herself, once she had slung the
stench-filled socks into the dispop. She busied herself in
the kitchen, punching out a scrumptious frappé dessert for
Carl's dinner. His last dinner on this Earth. Or anywhere.

Not that he'd notice, the big boob, not that he'd notice.

Nor did *she* notice the great wrinkle in one end of the
Deadly Nightshade. Caused by the prodding of the
broom.

He was yawning, and it looked like the eroded south
forty getting friendly.

"Jezus, Madge honey, I nearly overslept. Why'tcha
wake me? I'll be late for my shift."

She gawked, stricken. Twice!

"I ain't never seen nothin' like it, honey. I was enjoyin'
the best sleep of my life, but this here bright, real bright
streak of light was in my dreams, y'know? An' I couldn't
rest easy, y'know. I kept squintin' and tossin' and finally
hadda get up, cause I mean, Jeezus, it was painful.
Piercin', y'know? So I got up, an' a lucky thing, too, or
I'd'a missed my shift. Whyn'tcha wake me, huh?"

She mumbled a reply, her face hot and her hands constantly at her mouth; she had the urge to clamp down
hard with her teeth, to keep from shrieking.

She continued to mumble, punched out a hurried breakfast, and summarily ushered him off to his expressway.

Then she sank into a chair and had a good, deep cry.

Later, when she was certain she had control of herself,
she got out the pamphlet again.

This time there was no mistaking the annoyance in the pamphlet's voice.

"You failed again. I can tell from your emanations. Very seldom does anyone need two of the methods provided by our Kits . . . you are the first one in nearly 8,000 Kits that has needed all three. We hope you are proud of yourself."

"His dirty socks," she began, "I had to get them out . . ."

"I do not wish apologies. I want attention! The third method is very simple—even a dunce—"

"There's no need to get nasty about it!" she interrupted.

"—even a *dunce* cannot fail with it," the booklet plowed on ruthlessly. "Take out the last article contained in the Kit. The heart-globe. Do *not* agitate it as it is a sympathetic stimulator of the heartbeat—"

Then the sound came to Madge, and the knowledge that someone was near. Listening. She flipped the pamphlet closed, but it was too late.

Much too late.

Carl stood at the door. He showed his decaying teeth in a brown smile without humor. "I came back," he said. "Felt so damn tired'n beat I just couldn't go to work . . ."

She could feel the tiny muscles jumping all through her body.

"So that's what's been goin' on, huh Madge? I shoulda guessed you'd get up the guts one day soon. I'll haveta think back an' see if I can figger out what this Kit included. It'll be fun. My three was real wowzers, y'know."

She stared at him, uncomprehending. Had he found her Kit and had she not noticed?

"I recanize the pamphlet," he explained with a wave of his meaty hand. "I sent for one of them things over three months ago." His voice altered with incredible swiftness. Now casual and defacing, now harsh and bitter as sump water. "But how'n a hell could I of used it around someone like you . . . you'd of noticed the first lousy little trap that I'd'a set . . . you'd of vacuumed an' swept an' pried an' found it.

"I know you've hated me—but Gawd A'mighty, how I've hated *you!* You straighten an' pick an' fuss till . . ." he summed it all up, and ended it all, eleven years of it, ". . . till a guy can't even come home an' enjoy a belch!"

He smiled again . . . this time with dirty mirth. "Your goddamn floor's gonna get filthy today, Madge." He drew out the long, shiny knife. "Had one of the guys in Steel Molding make this for me . . . a *real* do-it-yourself."

Then there was pain and a feeling of incompleteness and she saw the blood begin to drip on the rug that she had kept so immaculate. A great deal of blood, a sea of blood, so much blood.

Madge Rubichek had been a methodical woman . . . So she could not check the dying statement that came bubbling to her lips:

"There's . . . a . . . double . . . money . . . back . . ."

His voice came from far away. "I know," he said.

ARGENT BLOOD

April 13: Today I made a discovery. I was allowed to look in the mirror in Doctor Mesh's office. I'm about forty years old, judging from my face and hair. I failed to recognize me, and by this I mean there is apparently no correlation between what I saw of me in the mirror and this trick memory of mine. But it's good to see one's face, although my own appears ordinary enough.

I must admit to more interest in the pretty bottles on Doctor Mesh's shelves than my face. Somewhere in dreams I remember bottles like those. I wanted the bottles so badly that a whirling came in my head. But I didn't try to take them, as I suspected that Doctor Mesh was watching closely.

Doctor Mesh said, "You're improving. Soon we'll give you the run of our little hospital and grounds, except, of course, the disturbed room." He pinched me on the arm playfully. "Have to keep you healthy."

I nodded and was delighted and the sickness inside went away. Then I could take my eyes off the shelves of bottles—nice ones full of good poisons—some that I recognized vaguely, others that struck no chord.

There would be another time.

Later I went back into the small ward—my home—the only one I really remember. Miss Utz smiled at me from her desk and I lay on my bed and watched her. She has strange, bottomless eyes. When I see her, the longing to be normal again is strongest. But the disturbances recur.

My ward is done in calm colors. The whole effect is soporific. I'm sure I never slept so much or dreamed so much. Bottles, bottles.

The food is good and I eat a great deal. My weight seems to remain fairly constant, decreasing when I'm disturbed, coming back to normal when released.

My fellow patients are not so well off. Most of them are very old and either idiotic or comatose. Only the man with the beard is rational enough to talk to sometimes.

The bearded man saw me watching him. "Pet!" he yelled at me. He makes me very angry sometimes. He's always saying that to me when he's disturbed. I wonder what he means?

I shall quit writing for the day. Doctor Mesh says it's good to keep a diary, but I'm afraid someone will read this. That would anger me, and extreme anger brings on disturbances.

I'm sleepy now.

April 18: I've got to stop this sort of thing. I tried again with the bearded man, but he won't drink water that he hasn't freshly drawn. I think he suspected that I'd done something, because he watched me malevolently for a long time.

I came out of the disturbed room yesterday, sick and weak, remembering nothing of that time.

No one seems to have found the bottle I hid the day I became disturbed, a bottle empty now down to the skull and crossbones, but to no purpose except the bearded man's anger. I wonder why Doctor Mesh angers me so? And Miss Utz? I guess it must be because they move and talk and exist. The old ones who don't move and talk to me don't anger me—only the bearded man and Doctor Mesh and Miss Utz.

But nothing seems to work on the Doctor or Miss Utz and the bearded man is very careful.

Today, at mid-morning, Miss Utz helped me down to the solarium and I sat there for a while. Outside, the flowers have begun to bloom and some minute purple and green creepers are folding their way over the walls around this tiny asylum. They look very good and poisonous.

My neck itched and I scratched at the places until they bled and Miss Utz laughed her cold laugh and put antiseptic on my neck. She told me that this is a private asylum run on private funds, taking no patients but hopeless ones that have been confined elsewhere for years before transfer here. If that is completely so, then why am I here?

In the afternoon Doctor Mesh tested my reflexes and listened to my heart. He says I'm in good physical condition. He seemed happy about that. He was evasive when I asked him if I'd ever be well, and that made me angry. I managed to hide all outward signs of my feeling.

When I was back in the ward and Miss Utz was temporarily out of sight, the feel of the poison bottle comforted me.

April 30: The dreams are growing worse. So clear and real. I dreamed I was in Doctor Mesh's office. I could see the pretty bottles on the shelves. Miss Utz and Doctor Mesh were reading my diary and laughing. The bearded man kept screaming at me from far away. The dream was very real, but my eyes would not open.

This morning the bearded man is watching me from his bed. He looks very weak, but he had a disturbance this week. Being disturbed is very hard on one, Doctor Mesh once told me.

I was in Doctor Mesh's office for a while earlier and got to look in the mirror. I did not recognize me again. Sometimes I feel as if my head had been cut open, the contents scrambled, and then recapped. There is no pain, but there is no place to search for things.

A little while ago I tried something from the new bottle that I'd taken from Doctor Mesh's office. It didn't work. Nothing works—even though I saw Miss Utz drink some of the water.

May 2: I shall have to hide this diary. I'm almost sure they are reading it. They brought the bearded man back from "disturbed" today. His eyes are red and sunken and he kept watching me all morning. When Miss Utz left the ward he beckoned me over with an insistent finger.

He said nothing. Instead he lifted his beard away and pointed at his throat. I looked at it, but could see nothing but some small, red marks, as if he'd cut himself with his fingernails. He pulled one of the cuts open with hands that shook and a tiny driblet of blood pulsed out. He laughed.

I looked away, the blood making me feel ill.

The corner of one of the pages in this diary is torn. I didn't tear it.

May 3: I talked to the bearded man today—if talk can describe the conversation we had. He's insistent. He said I can't know when they feed on me as I'm in a sort of seizure and that I'm their "pet" because I'm young and strong. He made me check my neck and there are red marks on it. He said they let me steal the poisons because they know I can't harm them.

He told me I killed three people outside, poisoned them. He says I was a pharmacist outside, but now I'm incurably insane and can't ever be released. He said I was in a state hospital for years before I came here. I don't remember it.

He claims that Doctor Mesh and Miss Utz are vampires.

I went back to my bed when he let me get away and spent a fairly restful afternoon. I dreamed of bottles on the shelf and something came to me in the dream—a thing all perfect like myself.

The bearded man says that we could kill them with silver bullets, but the thought of a gun is abhorrent to me.

I've never really believed in that sort of thing, but what if the bearded man is right? What if Doctor Mesh and Miss Utz are vampires. This place would be perfect for them. No investigation of death, no legal troubles, patients forgotten years ago. Take only the incurables, the forgotten. A regular supply.

But the plan, so intricate and perfect. I will have to have the bearded man's help. He will have to steal the things I want. If they are watching me, laughing when I steal from them, it would be too risky for me to take it.

May 4: We began the plan today. The bearded man managed to steal the large bottle of saline solution and the tube and needle to introduce it into the veins. He also managed the other part. The chemical was where I'd described it as being on Doctor Mesh's shelves. I even had the color of the bottle right. Now we must wait for the right time. Perhaps tonight?

I shall hide this book well.

May 6: I am in fever. We did not manage until last

night, and it took a very long time. I feel all steamy inside and there is a dizziness.

I'm trying for anger and a disturbance. Miss Utz is watching from her desk, her eyes hot and bright.

They will take me to the disturbed room.

May 9: A few lines. I'm ill. Nothing seems to be working inside me and the heat is such that my eyes see more brightness than shade. I'm in the disturbed room and I've seen no one alive all day. I can hear the bearded man's whiny laugh, and once I heard him clap his hands.

I think they are dead. They must be dead.

We put the silver chloride in the saline solution and put the needle in my arm and let it all flow inside. When I was disturbed they must have fed on me.

If I rise up I can see the toe of a female foot right at the door and it's all curled and motionless. I can't see Doctor Mesh, but he must be there in the hall near Miss Utz.

Dead of my poisoned blood, my fine and intricate blood. A new specific for vampires. *Silver Blood*.

I wish this heat would go away. Three outside and two in here. I want there to be time for more . . .

LORD RANDY, MY SON

He rebelled on the night the call came to leave the warm and liquid place; but in that way he was weak and nature was strong. Outside, the rains came; a storm so formidable that forecasters referred to it for all of the time that was left. He fought to remain with the mother-thing, but the

*mother-thing expelled him and in fear and rage he hurt
the mother-thing subtly. Black clouds hid the stars and
the trees bent only to the wind.*

The night before, Sam Moore had let his son, Randy,
play late in the yard—if "play" it was. The boy had no formal games and the neighborhood children shunned the
area of the Moore house. Sometimes a child would yell at
the boy insultingly from some hidden place, but mostly
now they stayed away.

Sam sat in the chaise longue and watched dully,
trapped in the self-pity of writing his own obituary, asking the timeless questions: Who were you? What did you
ever do? And why me? Why me now?

He watched the child with concealed revulsion. Randall moved quietly along the back line of hedges, his
small boy eyes watchful of the other yards that bordered
his own. There had been a time when it was a fetish with
the neighbor children to fling a rock when passing, before
the two Swihart boys, running away after disposing of
their missiles, had fallen into a well no one had even
known existed in the corner lot. Too bad about them, but
Randall lived with the remembrance of the rocks and appeared to distrust the amnesty. Sam watched as the boy
continued his patrol.

The pain within had been worse on that day and Sam
longed for the forgetfulness of sleep.

Finally it was time.

*The first one came in silence and the memories of that
night are lost in time. That one grew easily and alone, for
only later life is chronicled. His people migrated and
memory flickered into a mass of legends. But the blood
was there.*

Item: The old man had gardened in the neighborhood
for several years. He was a bent man with a soft, broken-

toothed smile, bad English, and a remembrance of things
past: swastikas, yellow stars, Buchenwald. Now and then
he wrote simple poems and sent them to the local newspaper, and once they had printed one. He was a friendly
old man and he spoke to everyone, including one of the
teenage neighborhood queens. She chose to misunder-
stand him and reported his friendliness as something
more.

On that day, a year gone now, the old man had been
digging at rosebushes in the front yard of the house
across the street. Randall had watched, sucking at a pep-
permint stick the old man had given him, letting the juice
run from the corners of his mouth.

The black car had squealed to a stop and the three pur-
poseful boys gotten out. They wore yellow sweaters. On
the back of each sweater an eagle had been cunningly
worked into the material so that the woven wings seemed
to take new flight as shoulders moved. Each boy carried a
chain-saw band with a black taped handle. Randall
watched them with growing interest, not really understanding yet.

They beat the old man with powerful, tackle-football
arms, and he had cowered away, crying out in a guttural,
foreign tongue. It was over quickly. The old man lay
crumpled and bleeding in the rich, dark dirt. The boys
piled back into the black car and peeled away at high
speed. Randall could hear the sounds of their laughter,
like pennants fluttering after them.

Two blocks away the land was not suitable for building. There was a steep hill. The tire blew there and the
black car went over the hill gaining speed. It cartwheeled
down, spouting enormous geysers of flame, a miniature
ferris wheel gone mad; and fire gushed out with an overpowering roaring sound that *almost* blocked out the
screams.

In the morning Sam Moore awoke unrefreshed. On that
Saturday the housekeeper-babysitter came on time for a

change and he left them sitting in the family room. The television was blaring a bloody war movie, where men died in appalling numbers. Randall was seated, legs crossed, on the floor in front of the television, watching avidly. Mrs. Cable watched the screen and refused to meet Sam's glance, lost in her own bitter world. There'd been a time when Sam had issued instructions before leaving, but those days were gone. Not very many women would care for a retarded child. Now, enmeshed in his own problem, and really not caring much, he said little. If the watching was casual and the safety of the boy only probable . . . he had still carried out the formal, social necessities of child care.

He looked at the boy and something within him darkened. Ann had been brilliant and her pregnancy had been normal; but the birth had been difficult and the boy a monstrous problem. She had changed. The boy had not. Early tests on him had been negative, but physically there had always been a lack of interest, slow movement, eyes that could track and follow, but did not.

He could not force himself to approach the boy this morning.

"Good-bye," he said, and received a brief look upward with minor recognition involved. A boy is only three once; but what happens when he is three and eight at the same time? When he will be three forever?

On the television screen a dark-skinned soldier dragged his white captain from the path of an onrushing tank. Sam remembered the script. It was one of Hollywood's message films. Comradeship would continue until the dark-skinned one needed another kind of help.

Outside, he failed to notice the loveliness of the day. He stood in front of the garage and considered. (With the rolling door down, the garage was tight. He could start the car and it would be easy. That was what Ann, his wife, had done, but for a different reason and in a different way. She'd swallowed a box of sleeping pills when he was out of town trying a case. That had been a long time ago after the hospitals and clinics, after the last of the faith healers with their larcenous, sickening morality, the confident, grasping herbalists, the slick charlatans and quacks to whom, in desperation, she'd taken the boy. Four years now. No one had examined Randall since.

(She'd never been really *there* after Randall was born. She'd wandered on for a while, large, sensitive eyes looking out from some faraway place, her mind a cluttered dustbin of what might have been.

("Just don't touch me," she had said. "I know they said we ought to have another, but don't. . . . Please, Sam." And that which was still partially alive in him had died. He knew it was the boy. Now . . . it wasn't that he'd not loved her, but he could recall her face only in the boy's face, in that small and hateful visage, that face that had killed the thing Sam loved.)

He rolled up the garage door with a clang, and drove to his law office. Another day, perhaps another dollar. There weren't many days left now. Dr. Yancey had said sixmonthstoayear, and that had been more than four months ago; on the day they had opened Sam Moore and quickly sutured him again to hide the corrupt mass inside.

"Too far along," Yancey had said, and then added the old words of despair that many men finally hear: "Nothing we can do."

Siddharta Gautama came easily in the park with the remembrance of elephants. Legends say that the trees bowed to him. His mother, Maya, felt sustained by an intense feeling of power. The blood was strong, but the child was slow and sheltered and the fulfillment never reached, the gift grown into vagueness, never fully used.

Item: Randall sat under a tree in front of the Moore house. He watched the world around him with curious intensity. A honey bee flew near and he watched the creature with some concern, but it did not attack. They didn't bother him much since that one had stung him in the spring, and he'd destroyed them all for a ten-block radius.

He could hear the loud noise long before he could tell from where it came. A sound truck blared close by. In a few moments it came to Randall's corner and slowed. On its side there was a garish picture of a man in priestly robes holding a rifle in front of his chest, eyes flashing fire. The sign below said: "Father Tempest Fights Communism." Music boomed over the speakers, decibels above the permitted limits. Randall held his ears. The sound hurt.

The driver cut the music back and turned up the volume for his hand microphone. "Big rally tonight!" he called. "Hear Father Tempest save the world and tell YOU how to fight the infiltrators who would destroy us. High school gym, seven o'clock." The voice took on a threatening note. "Don't let your neighbors be there without you." In the other seat beside the driver, a man in priestly robes smiled and made beneficent gestures as people came to doors and windows.

Overhead there were sudden clouds and a few drops of rain fell. Lightning bolted from the sky, missed the tall trees, and made a direct hit on the sound truck. Silence came and Randall removed his hands from his ears. People ran into the street and, in a while, Randall could hear a siren.

He left the front yard and went to the window at the side. From there he could see Mrs. Cable. She had managed somehow to sleep through it all. Her mouth hung open and she snored with an easy rhythm. The television was still on, hot with a soap opera now.

Randall began to pace the back hedge fence, guarding it. There'd been one boy who appeared friendly and would smile at Randall and then slyly do little things of pinching and hitting when no one watched. That was the boy with the BB gun, who shot the squirrel that took the bits of food from Randall's hand, the boy who killed one of the fish in the fishpond. The squirrel still lived, but it was more cautious now. And there were still three fish in the pond. There had always been three, except for that one day. One of the fish now was not quite the same color and shape as the others.

The big dog came into the yard through the hedge and they frisked together.

Randall smiled at the dog. "Nice dog," he said. A stump of tail waved in adoration.

Sam spent a dreary day in the office, snapping at his secretary, being remote to clients. Now he was not as busy as he'd once been. He refused cases that might drag. Partly it was the alien thing that grew inside, but partly— and he had a sort of sullen pride about it—there was the matter of being too good at his job. He'd surrounded himself with that job when Ann had gone, merged into it. Now he refused the proffered retainers to defend or prosecute that which he knew he wouldn't live to see. It was a minor, ethical point, but a man takes greater cognizance of minor points when he begins to die.

His own decisions grew harder to make, and clients read it in his eyes and voice. The motley mob that had once invaded his office fell to a whisper, and soon there was time.

He thought about the boy. He knew he'd ignored the child after Ann's death, and worse, he'd hated the boy, relating it back to Ann, knowing that her suicide was a product of what the boy was.

The newspaper offered escape. The world grew more sour daily and so seemed easier to leave. Today two more countries had quit the United Nations. Sweden reported increased fallout. There was indecisiveness over a new test ban. Two African nations announced the development of their own bombs. In Mississippi a member of a fanatical white organization had shot and killed a circuit judge who'd sentenced nine men accused and convicted of lynching a civil rights worker. In his own state an amendment to the state constitution outlawing the death penalty had lost by a wide margin.

On the way home there was an ache in his back that had never been there before.

Ching-tsai dreamed deeply on the night of coming. The chilin appeared to her. She dreamed and missed the dragons that walked the quiet skies. Once again the child was slow and sheltered and kept apart.

Item: Mrs. Cable slept on. Keeping away from prime time, which was reserved for westerns, giveaway shows, comedies and the like, the television presented a program on a housing development in New York. They showed the tenements that were being replaced; they showed the narrow streets and the tired and dirty people. Cameras cleverly watched as the buildings came down and high-rise, low-rent apartments were built. The reporter's voice was flat and laconic. Crime continued in the rebuilt area. The favorite now was to catch the rent collector in the elevator, strip him, and jam small change up his rectum. Rape increased, for the apartments were better soundproofed than the old tenements.

Randall watched. The people still looked tired and dirty.

After the documentary there was another soap opera. Mrs. Cable came awake and they watched together. This one was about a man and woman who were in love and who were married, but unfortunately not to each other.

The house was hot and empty. Sam went to the open window and saw them. Mrs. Cable was stretched out on the chaise longue, a paper held over her eyes to block the fierce sun. Randall was at the goldfish pond that Sam had constructed in a happier year. Three hardy goldfish had outlived the last harsh winter and the indifferent spring. What they subsisted on, Sam could not guess. He knew that *he* didn't feed them.

The boy held small hands over the pool and Sam watched covertly. It was as if the child felt Sam's eyes on him, for he turned his head and smiled directly at the window. Then he turned again to the pool, trailing quick hands in the water. The right one came up gently grasping a goldfish. The boy passed it from hand to hand, and the hand sought another.

It was something that Sam had never seen before, but the boy did it with an air, as if it were an often-repeated act.

Randall had an affinity for animals. Sam remembered the incident of the dog. The back neighbors owned a large and cantankerous German shepherd that had been a neighborhood terror since acquisition. Once, when Randall made one of his periodic runaways, Sam had come upon the boy huddled against the dog. Sam stood watching, half expecting the animal, which its owners normally kept carefully chained, to rend and tear. But the dog made no overt move and only whined when Sam took the boy away.

Lately the dog's conduct must have improved with age, for Sam had seen it playing happily about the neighborhood.

He made up a check and took it out to Mrs. Cable. It paid her for the week and she took it with good grace. Payday was the only time she unbent and showed any real desire to talk.

"Lots of excitement," she said. "Lightning hit a truck right down the street. I was asleep, but Mrs. Taldemp was telling me. Two men killed." She shook her head in wonder. "Right down the street and I missed it." She nodded at Randall. "He's coming along. He does things he didn't used to do. Those mean little ones that used to throw rocks don't come close anymore. He used to try to run to them and give them his toys, but he just watches now if he sees one. They stay away when he's outside." She shook her head. "He still don't talk much, but sometimes he'll say something right out loud and clear when I ain't expecting it." She laughed her whinny laugh. "It's a shame nothing can be done for him. You still trying to get him in that state dumb school?"

Sam fought the pain inside. "Not much use," he said shortly. "They're full. He's way down the list to get in."

He escorted her to the front door. On most days she kept conversation to a minimum, but today she wouldn't run down.

"He's sure quick. There's a squirrel up in one of them trees. I turned my back and he was up there feeding it. I thought you said that old elm was rotten?"

Sam nodded. Every movement sent a wave of pain up his back.

"Well, he climbed up it and I had a dickens of a time getting him down. Don't seem rotten to me," she grumbled.

It was rotten. It had died this spring and never come out in leaves. Sam could see it vaguely out the back window. The other trees were in full leaf. He imagined that he could see buds and small leaves on the elm, but he knew he must be wrong.

He finally got Mrs. Cable out the door and called Doc Yancey. When that was done he eased gingerly into a chair. The pain receded slightly. The boy sat on the floor watching him with a child's curious intentness, head cocked slightly, completely without embarrassment. Sam admitted to himself that the boy was handsome. His features were regular, his body wiry and strong. Once Sam had visited the State Mentally Retarded Home and the eyes of the children there were what he most remembered. Most of those eyes had been dull and without luster. A few of the eyes had been foolers. Randall's eyes were foolers. They were bright with the brightness of cold snow, but they lacked involvement with the world around him.

"You hurt, Father?" Randall questioned. He made a tiny gesture with one hand, as if he were testifying and had found a sudden truth and was surprised by it. "You hurt, Father," he said again. He pointed out the window. "All hurt," he said.

"Yes," Sam said. "The whole world hurts."

The boy turned away as Sam heard the car in the drive. It was Dr. Yancey. The man came in with brisk steps and Sam had a moment of quick, consuming hatred for the other man; the solid, green envy of the sick for the well.

Dr. Yancey spoke first to the boy. "Hello, Randy. How are you today?"

For a moment Sam did not think the boy would answer.

Randall looked at the doctor without particular interest. "I am young," he said finally, in falsetto.

"He says that sometimes to people," Sam said. "I think he means he's all right."

Yancey went into the kitchen and brought back water and a yellow capsule. "This won't put you under." He handed the capsule and water to Sam and Sam downed them dutifully. He let Yancey help him from the chair to the couch. Expert fingers probed him. The boy watched with some interest.

"You're swollen, but there aren't any real signs of serious organ failure. You really ought to be in a hospital."

"Not yet," Sam said softly. "There's the boy." He looked up at Yancey. "How long, Doc?" He asked it not really wanting to know and yet wanting to know.

"Not very long now, Sam. I think the cancer's spread to the spine." He kept his voice low and turned to see if the boy was listening.

Randall got up from the floor. He moved quietly and gracefully out of the room and down the hall. A light clicked on in the study.

"He's sort of unnerving," Sam said. "He'll go back in the study and get down books and turn pages. I've got a good encyclopedia back there and some medical books I use in damage cases. I suppose he likes the pictures. Sometimes he spends hours back there."

Some say Ubu'l Kassim destroyed his father two months before the coming. The shock of death and birth weakened the mother-thing and she died a few years after. His life was confused, moving from relative to relative, slow maturation. Something within him hid from the world until early manhood.

Item: The books were puzzling. There was so much in them that was so clearly wrong, but they were not cruel of themselves, only stupid and careless. He remembered the mother-thing and wondered why he had hurt her. The father-thing was hurt also, but he had not done that. There was no love in the father-thing, but the father-thing had never hurt him.

The books were no help.

Alone, unaided by what the world had become and what it meant to him, he made his decision. He made it for the one time and the one thing, putting the rest back, delaying.

The pill was effective for a few hours and then it began to wear off. He took another and checked the boy. Randall lay in his bed, small body lost in covers, breathing slowly, evenly, his eyes open.

"Where is the mother?" he asked.

There were two feelings. Sam had the desire to destroy the boy and an equal feeling to catch the child up and hold him close. He did neither. He rearranged the covers.

"She's gone far away," he said softly to the boy.

Randall nodded.

Sam straightened the study. The boy had been at his books again. He put them back on the shelves. He went to his own bed. Sleep came quickly.

Outside, in the neighborhood, most lights were still on. People stared uneasily at their television screens. There was another confrontation, this time in the Near East. Hands moved closer to the red button, the button that man had made. The President spoke and tensions eased, for some. The world, for what it was and what all men had made it, would remain for a while.

For Sam there was a dream.

The faces of a thousand clients came and blended into one sick and ignorant and prejudiced face, a "never-had" and "never-will" face that whined the injustice of life as it spawned children to be supported by the myriad public doles. It was a face that Sam knew well, a face that pleaded for divorce and demanded alimony and plotted rape and confessed murder. It was a face that hated all minorities and majorities of which it was not the leading member, that cursed fate and defrauded welfare. Partly the face was familiar and he knew it, for it was his own face.

It was a dream built of fifteen years of practice. It was not a nightmare, for it was far better than life.

The dream fit life though, and at the moment of dreaming, if he could have made a rational choice, if the instinct for life had not been so strong and inbred, he would have chosen death.

He came almost to wakefulness once, but he slid back into the well where there was only one tiny circle of light. Ann and the boy were there. They touched him with soft hands. He turned them into the circle of life and their faces could be seen and those faces bore the same marks as his client-self face, cruel, sick, angry, and in pain. Their hands still touched him and he writhed to escape, revolted at the touch. With horrible pain and with tearing and burning he retched the gorge within him away.

He awoke.

Only one pair of hands was real.

Randall stood by the bed. The boy's hands were laid lightly across the bed, resting and unmoving on Sam's chest. There was something in the boy's face, an awareness, a feeling. Sam could not read it all, but there was satisfaction and accomplishment and perhaps even love. Then expression wandered away. The boy yawned and removed his hands. He walked away and Sam soon heard the rustle of the silk comforter from the boy's bedroom.

A spasm of empty pain came. Sam got up weakly and made it to the kitchen and took another pill and sat for a while on the couch until it took effect. He came back past the boy's room and looked in. Randall lay straight in bed. There was a bright sheen of sweat on the child's forehead. His eyes were open, watching and waiting.

"I am young," the child said again, plaintively and to no one.

"Yes," Sam said softly. "So very young."

"There was a head thing," Randall said slowly, searching for words. "Hurt doggy." He reached a small finger out and laid it on Sam's wrist. "Fish always hungry. I gave to them." He shook his head. "See words. Can't say them." Confidence came in his voice. "I will grow more quickly now." He moved his hands off Sam's wrist and closer to the abdomen. "All gone now. All gone every place," he said, and the look of Sam's bedroom came fleetingly again.

Sam watched without comprehension.

The cold, lost eyes watched him and the next words turned Sam's blood cold. The boy's voice came up in volume and with a ferocity that Sam had never heard before. "See things on teevee, read them in the books and papers, so many bad things, all hate out there like others hate me." He touched his own small head. "So many things in here not ready yet." The eyelids closed tight and a tiny tear came at each corner. "Not sorry. I will grow older," Randall said, his voice a cruel, unhuman promise.

There was Another who was born in a manger and died on a cross. That One was sheltered for a while and maturity was unforced.

But the new One, the One born for our times, would see man's consuming hate of all others, so consuming that the hate extends even to himself. See it in the close world around Him. See it on television and read of it in the

*newspapers and then grow unsheltered in this world of
mass and hysterical communication.*

Then plan. Then decide.

This One would come to maturity and ripen angry.

SHUT THE FINAL DOOR

The night was gentle and so Willie sat out on the combination fire escape and screened play area that hung in
zigzags from the north side of the government-built, low-
rent apartment building. He stayed out there in his
wheelchair for a long time watching the world of lights
from the other buildings around him. He liked the night.
It softened the savage world, so that he could forget the
things he saw and did in the day. Those things still
existed, but darkness fogged them.

He reached around, fumbling under his shirt, and let
his hand touch the long scar where it started. He couldn't
reach all of it for it ran the width of his back, a slanting
line, raised from the skin. Sometimes it ached and there
was a little of that tonight, but it wasn't really bad anymore. It was only that he was dead below the scar line,
that the upper half of him still lived and felt, but the
lower felt nothing, did nothing.

Once they'd called him Willie the Runner, and he had
been very fast: the running a defense from the cruel
world of the apartments, a way out, a thing of which he'd
been quite proud. That had been when he was thirteen.
Now he was fifteen. The running was gone forever and
there was only a scar to remind him of what had been
once. But the new gift had come, the one the doctors had

hinted about. And those two who'd been responsible for the scar had died.

A cloud passed across the moon and a tiny, soft rain began to fall. He wheeled off the fire escape and into the dirty hall. It was very dark inside. Someone had again removed the light bulbs from their receptacles. Piles of refuse crowded the corners and hungry insects scurried at the vibration of Willie's wheelchair. In the apartment his mother sat in front of the television. Her eyes were open, but she wasn't seeing the picture. She was on something new, exotic. He'd found one of the bottles where she'd carefully hidden it. Dilaudin, or something like that. It treated her well. He worked the wheelchair over to the television and turned off the late-night comic, but she still sat there, eyes open and lost, looking intently at the darkened tube. He went on into his own bedroom, got the wheelchair close to the bed, and clumsily levered himself between the dirty sheets.

He slept and sleeping brought the usual dreams of the days of fear and running. In the dream they laughed coldly and caught him in the dark place and he felt the searing pain of the knife. He remembered the kind doctor in the hospital, the one who kept coming back to talk to him, the one who talked about compensation and factors of recovery. The doctor had told him his arms might grow very strong and agile. He'd told him about blind men who'd developed special senses. He'd smiled and been very nice, and Willie had liked him. The gift he'd promised had come. Time passed in the dream and it became better and Willie smiled.

In the morning, before his mother left for the weekly ordeal with the people at the welfare office, Willie again had her wheel him down to the screened play area and fire escape. In the hall, with the arrival of day, the smell was stifling, a combination of dirt and urine and cooking odors and garbage. The apartments in the building were almost new, but the people who inhabited the apartments

had lived in tenement squalor for so long that they soon
wore all newness away. The tenants stole the light bulbs
from the hallways, used dark corners as toilets of conven-
ience, discarded the leftovers of living in the quickest
easiest places. And they fought and stole and raped and,
sometimes, killed.

Sometimes, Willie had seen a police car pass in the
streets outside, but the policemen usually rode with eyes
straight ahead and windows rolled up tight. On the few
times that police came into the apartment area they came
in squads for their own protection.

Outside the air was better. Willie could see the other
government apartments that made up the complex, and if
he leaned forward he could, by straining, see the early
morning traffic weaving along the expressway by the faraway river.

His mother frowned languidly at the sky, her choco-
late-brown face severe. "It'll maybe rain," she said, slur-
ring the words together. "If it rains you get back in,
hear?"

"Okay," he said, and then again, because he was never
sure she heard him, "Okay!" He looked at her swollen,
sullen face, wanting to say more, but no words came. She
was so very young. He'd been born almost in her child-
hood and there was within him the feeling that she re-
sented him, hated caring for him, abominated being tied
to him, but did the dreary duty only because there was no
one else and because the mother-feeling within warred
with all the other wants and drives and sometimes won an
occasional victory. Willie remembered no father, and his
mother had never spoken of one.

"None of them bad kids bother you up here, do they?"
she asked, always suspicious.

He smiled, really amused. "No," he said.

She shook her head tiredly and he noticed the twitch in
the side of her dark face. She said, "Some of them's bad
enough to bother around a fifteen-year-old boy in a
wheelchair. Bad enough to do 'most anything I guess.

When we moved in here I thought it would be better."
She looked up at the sky. "It's worse," she ended softly.

Willie patiently waited out her automatic ministrations,
the poking at the blanket around his wasting legs, the
peck on the forehead. Finally, she left.

For a while then he was alone and he could crane and
watch the expressway and the river and the downtown to
the north. He could hear the complex around him come to
angry life, the voices raised in argument and strife. Down
below four boys came out of a neighboring building.
They were dressed alike, tight jeans, brown jackets, hair
long. He saw them gather in front of the building and one
of them looked up and saw him watching. That one
nudged the others and they all looked up, startled, and
they went away like deer, around the far corner of their
building at a quick lope. Willie only nodded.

A block away, just within his vision, a tall boy came out
of the shadows and engaged another boy in a shouting argument. A small crowd gathered and watched indolently,
some yelling advice. Willie watched with interest. When
the fight began they rolled out of sight and Willie could
only see the edges of the milling crowd and soon lost interest in watching.

The sun came out and the sky lightened and Willie felt
more like facing the day. He looked down at his legs
without real sorrow. Regret was an old acquaintance, the
feeling between them no longer strong. Willie leaned
back in the wheelchair. With trained ears alert to any sudden sound of danger, he dozed lightly.

Memory again became a dream. When he had become
sure of the gift he had followed them to their clubhouse.
It was in a ruined building that the city was tearing down
to build more of the interminable housing units. He rolled
right up to the door and beat on it boldly and they came
and he saw the surprise on their faces and their quick
looks to see if he'd brought police along.

"Hello, Running Willie, you crippled bastard," the one

who'd wielded the knife said. The one who'd held him and watched smiled insolently.

He sat there alone in the chair and looked back at them, hating them with that peculiar, complete intensity, wanting them dead. The sickness came in his stomach and the whirling in his head and he saw them move at him before the sunlit world went dark brown.

Now they were dead.

A door opened below and Willie came warily awake. He looked down and saw Twig Roberts observing the day.

"Okay to come on up, Willie?" Twig asked carefully.

"Sure," Willie said negligently.

Twig came up the stairs slowly and sat down on the top one, looking away into the distance, refusing to meet Willie's eyes. He was a large, dark boy, muscled like a wrestler, with a quick, foxy face. He lived in the apartment below Willie's.

"What we goin' to do today, Willie boy?" Twig asked it softly, his voice a whine. "Where we headin'?" He continued to look out at the empty sky and Willie knew again that Twig feared him. A small part of Willie relished the fear and fed on it, and Willie knew that the fear diminished both of them.

Willie thought about the day. Once the trips, the forays, into that wild, jackdaw land below had been an exciting thing, a thing of danger. That had been when the power was unsure and slow, but the trips were as nothing now. Instead of finding fear below he brought it.

He said softly, "We'll do something, Twig." Then he nodded, feeling small malice. "Maybe down at Building Nineteen. You been complaining about Building Nineteen, ain't you?" He smiled, hiding the malice. "You got someone down there for me?"

Twig looked at him for the first time. "You got it wrong, Willie. I got relatives in that building. I never even taken you around there for fear . . ." He stopped and then went on. "There's nothing wrong with Nineteen.". He watched earnestly until Willie let his smile widen. "You were puttin' me on, Willie," Twig said, in careful half-reproach.

"Sure, Twig," Willie said, closing his eyes and leaning back in the wheelchair. "We'll go down and just sort of look around."

The fan in the elevator didn't work and hadn't worked for a long time, but at least today the elevator itself worked. The odor in the shaft was almost overpowering and Willie was glad when they were outside in the bright sun that had eaten away the morning fog.

Twig maneuvered him out the back entrance of the building. Outside the ground was covered with litter, despite the fact that there were numerous trash receptacles. A rat wheeled and flashed between garbage cans and Willie shivered. The running rat reminded Willie of the days of fear.

They moved on along the sidewalks, Willie in the chair, Twig dutifully behind. Ahead of them Willie could almost feel the word spread. The cool boys vanished. The gangs hid in trembling fear, their zip guns and knives forgotten. Arguments quieted. In the graveled play yards the rough games suspended. Small children watched in wonder from behind convenient bushes, eyes wide. Willie smiled and waved at them, but no one came out. Once a rock came toward them, but when Willie turned there was no one to be seen. There was a dead zone where they walked. It was always like that these days.

A queer thought came to Willie as he rode along in solitary patrol. It was an odd thought, shiny and unreal. He wondered if someplace there was a someone with the gift of life, a someone who could set stopped breath to moving again, bring color back to a bloodless face, restart a failed heart, bring thought back to a dead mind. He rather hoped that such a gift existed, but he knew that on these streets such a gift wouldn't last. In this filth, in this world of murderous intent the life-giver would have been torn apart. If the life-giver was Willie—if that had been the gift—they would have jerked him from the moving casket he rode, stomped him, mutilated him. And laughed.

There were other worlds. Willie knew that dimly, without remembrance, without real awareness. There was only a kind of dim longing. He knew that the legs were the things that had saved him from a thousand dangers. He remembered the leering man who'd followed him one day when he was twelve, the one who wanted something, who touched and took. He remembered the angry ones with their knives and bicycle chains, the gangs that banded together to spread, rather than absorb, terror. He looked at his world: the ones who'd roll you for the price of a drink and the ones who'd kill you for a fix. It was the only world he knew. Downtown was a thing of minutes spent. It wasn't life. Life was here.

The legs had been survival. A knife had taken them. The doctor had promised something and Willie had believed. Survival was still necessary and the world savage.

So was the compensating gift.

Twig pushed on into a narrow alley between trash cans. The sound of their coming disturbed an old white man who was dirtily burrowing in one of the cans. He looked up at them, filthy hands still rooting in the can. His thin, knobby-armed body seemed lost in indecision between whether to dig deeper in the muck or take flight. Hunger won.

"What you doin' there, man?" Twig demanded, instantly pugnacious at the sight of the dirty, white face.

The old man stood his ground stubbornly and Willie felt an almost empathy with him, remembering hungry days. The man's old eyes were cunning, the head a turtle's head, scrawnily protruding up from its shell of filthy clothing. Those eyes had run a thousand times from imagined terror, but they could still calculate chances. Those

eyes saw only a boy in a wheelchair, a larger boy behind.

The old man reached in his pocket. "Ge' away, you li'l
black bassurds. Ge' away fum me." The hand came out
and there was a flash of dull metal. A knife.

Willie saw Twig smile triumphantly. Those who stood
their ground were hard to find in these days of increasing
fear.

"Hate him, Willie," Twig said softly. "Hate him
now!"

Willie smiled at the old man and hated him without
dislike. He had to concentrate very hard, but finally the
wrenching, tearing feeling came in his head and the
brownout and the sickness became all. He faded himself
into the hate and became one with it, and time stopped
until there was nothing. When it was done and he was
again aware he opened his eyes.

The old man was gone. There was nothing left to show
he'd ever existed, no clothes, no knife.

"Did he run?" Willie asked.

Twig shook his head. "He smoked," he said, smiling
hugely. "That was the best one yet. He smoked a kind of
brown smoke and there was a big puff of flame, and suddenly he ain't there anymore." He cocked his head and
clapped his hands in false exuberance. "That one was
good, Willie. It was sure good." He smiled a good smile
that failed to reach his eyes.

The sun was warm and Willie sat there and knew he'd
been alone for all fifteen of his years and now, with the
gift, that he could remain alone and that he was quite
sanely mad.

He looked again at the children playing their rough
games in the measured gravel and he knew he could ex-
plode them all like toy balloons, but the insanity he
owned, he realized, should be worse than that.

The sun remained warm and he contemplated it and

thought about it and wondered how far the gift extended. *If I should hate the sun . . .*

There was another thought. He worked it over in his head for a long time, while his fingers absently reached and stroked the long scar on his back.

There was a way out, a possible escape.

Tomorrow he might try hating himself.

THE DIFFERENCE

I confess freely that I am, by profession, a lawyer and most recently a circuit court judge. I am also a writer of mystery novels. I've been mixing law with writing mysteries since law school with some minor success.

As a judge I've found myself suspect among my peers. If I arise to present a viewpoint or appear on a panel at a meeting of the judiciary I'm invariably introduced by a smiler as a writer of mystery novels and, therefore, not to be taken seriously. On the other hand, in my capacity as a writer, when I lecture to those interested in the craft, there's always a preliminary, dark statement that I'm also a circuit court judge, so watch me carefully and admit nothing in my presence.

My writer friends are both curious and disturbed about my judgeship. When I was a mere lawyer I was a fount of free information for them, but now they watch me for outward signs of some inward tyranny and comment caustically to me about judges in general.

Recently I became involved in a late-night conversation with two of my acquaintances. One is a lawyer, the other is a writer.

Gladstone, the lawyer, is a full-blooded pragmatist. He habitually wears dark, careful suits and subdued shirts and ties. He talks incessantly about order of proof, closing arguments, and the *res gestae*. He has one glaring failing. He reads widely. He has even read some of my books.

Poechristie, the writer, is a Writer with a capital W. He's not yet been overly successful at selling his work, but he teaches a course in creative writing, reviews books for the local paper, and like that. Once, some years back, he got a low, three-figure advance from one of the lending library publishers for a suspense novel. It didn't sell enough copies to pay him any royalties beyond the advance. He affects a beard, wears Levi's and bright shirts with catchy pictures and mottos on them. He's a fanatical mystery reader. He believes devoutly in cryptic messages beside all dead bodies, visitors observed in the night, dogs that did or didn't bark. He's "working" on another book and has been these past five years.

We stared at our drinks. The bar, now that it was quite late, was silent around us.

Gladstone said, "Judge, I want you to know that I'm a bit ashamed of myself for filing that motion for change of venue from you when I prosecuted that last murder case. The problem was your mystery novels. I've read them, you know."

Poechristie examined Gladstone's neat suit with barely concealed contempt. They'd been at each other all evening, and I'd been the peacemaker, hoping they were both too well bred for it to become more than a game of insults.

"*You* prosecuted a murder case? Are you positive you tried the right man?"

Gladstone looked irritated and I said soothingly, "Come now, gentlemen." I then observed Gladstone with a jaundiced eye. "Why would my writing mysteries, even those you admit reading, be such a problem to you?"

Gladstone smiled. "I suppose the problem is that I

have read your stuff. Perry Mason things. A lawyer gets his client off."

"But I remember that last murder case you prosecuted, Gladstone. It was a cinch. You had eyewitnesses to the murder. The defendant had made open threats about the deceased before he killed him. You had the murder weapon and even a confession. The jury was only out something like fifteen minutes."

"Thirteen," Gladstone said proudly.

Poechristie watched us carefully, then placed one Levi-wrapped leg over the other. He said, "The whole thing sounds suspicious to me. A setup. Don't you remember, Judge, when you had the same sort of basic situation in *Song of Corpus Juris?* All the evidence was bad and there were eyewitnesses and a gun and all of that, but you caught the real killer finally. I mean, we must admit that just because all of the facts are against a poor defendant it doesn't mean that he or she committed the dirty deed." He nodded enthusiastically. "Not only did your man, Don Robak, get the supposed killer off and find the real one, but he wound up with the pretty girl, too. Not that the romance lasted long."

"That book wasn't supposed to parallel any real-life situation," I said, somewhat embarrassed.

Gladstone smiled. "I supposed I really should just give up reading your books and take pot luck in your court. But I remembered all of the books I'd read by you when I filed my motion for change of venue. I particularly remembered the one where you had the guy waiting up on death row and just a few days—hours—left. You knew the governor wasn't going to grant clemency and that all appeals had been about exhausted. Yet you still managed to get him off. That worried me. I thought maybe you'd have gotten similarly interested in the murder case I was scheduled to prosecute. I could foresee interminable hearings. You might have sent out, in the midst of trial, for experts to test the signature on the confession, fingerprinted it to see who else might have tampered with it. You might have become interested in angles from which the gun couldn't have been fired. You might have inquired into the eyewitnesses. Some of them were opposite politically from the defendant. I decided I just couldn't take a chance on you, Judge."

Poechristie had gone rigid while Gladstone rambled. "You mean to say that all of those things weren't done? It seems to me that someone should inquire into your ethics, Gladstone. I mean, after all, there are certain minimum limits." He nodded firmly. "The Judge here well knows that the only confession worth a hoot is one wherein the real killer thinks he's gotten away with it, except he's worried about this one guy, our hero of course, who he thinks is about to figure it out. So he therefore has to track down the hero and do away with him. He then boasts about how he's done the other kills. But unknown to him there are other people listening. *That's* a confession." He turned to me. "Like you did it in *The Poison Summer*, Judge."

I succeeded in remaining cool. I said, "You gentlemen just have to understand that I separate what I write from real life. My fiction wouldn't work in real life. Real life wouldn't work in my fiction."

Gladstone asked, "It wouldn't?"

Poechristie eyed me unbelievingly. Back behind the bar, a little away, the bartender had started to snore.

"No," I said. "Juries in trials see only the one case they have to try. Only an occasional juror isn't convinced, virtually from the start, that the defendant isn't guilty of the crime. Jurors see pictures of a body or bodies. They see weapons and listen to ballistic experts. They hear and inspect confessions. And there's the defendant, right in front of them in court, connected with all of the things they're seeing. It's duck soup normally. Right, Brother Gladstone?"

He nodded carefully. "Well, it isn't all exactly that easy."

I went determinedly on, "Besides, persons committing

crimes of violence usually do stupid things in their excitement and fear. Mostly, despite all the Miranda warnings in the world, they confess. Even when they don't confess they leave guns and shells and items of clothing behind. They use their own guns and they leave fingerprints. They panic and lie about obvious things to avoid suspicions and so are caught when their lies are found out."

"The whole thing sounds rather—unsporting—to me," Poechristie said, sniffing once or twice.

I turned to Gladstone. "You know that prosecutors don't bother to try most people they don't have strong cases against. They plea bargain them or dismiss them figuring they'll see the persons involved again."

"That's certainly right," Gladstone said, nodding.

Poechristie cut in triumphantly, "Then how come you didn't have the prosecutor do that in the one you had a judge for the hero in? *Rivertown Risk?* That was a weak case."

"Not that weak. And it was a kind of political thing. The prosecutor was after the presumed killer and was motivated partly by politics."

"Then no rule applies if there's politics involved?"

Poechristie and Gladstone both waited.

"Not exactly," I said, sounding a bit lame, but damned if I was going to try to explain politics. "What I'm trying to say is that the fiction I write differs markedly from the fact I see. In fiction you can get around almost anything—a confession, eyewitnesses, ballistics, things found near the body, even flight. In actual fact, I've never seen an accused get 'out of it' when very many of those things are present and provable. And I've never seen or heard of a lawyer unmasking the real killer in the midst of the trial of the accused."

Poechristie appeared crushed. "You're not saying for sure it never happened?" He was a great Gardner fan.

"I'm only saying I've never heard of it. I'll cheerfully admit that I've heard of about everything else. The law books which report the cases in my state and surrounding states are my best friends when I begin to plot a new novel. The things that people have actually done to each other are many times more peculiar than those concocted out of whole cloth in the fictions I write."

Poechristie smiled at Gladstone.

"See!" he said.

Gladstone nodded his head. "I suppose I'm convinced. Perhaps you can keep your life separated into two compartments." He nodded carefully. "Knowing that it can be done that way makes me want to sit down on my next vacation and dash off a mystery novel."

Poechristie looked at me and I looked back and nodded.

"Do that," we chorused mockingly together.

This last article was something I did for Dilys Winn and *Murder Ink,* her lovely collection. That book ran long and so "The Difference" was crowded out. Dilys' publisher had paid me, so now and here I'm having my cake and eating it too.

In this book there are three collaborative stories, one with Eugene DeWeese and two with Harlan Ellison. See the copyright page for further details. If these stories are flawed, then blame me and not my collaborators. The two above-named writers are extremely competent men, sometimes even inspired men. It was great fun working with them.

Some few of these stories get crosswise in science fiction/mystery. I make no excuse for them or that. When I began I read Bloch and Bradbury. As time went on I read Lovecraft and Hoch, Heinlein and Fred Brown. Now I read Ellin and John D. MacDonald, Westlake and Gordon Dickson. Ideas and stories happen without formal declarations of war.

I am what I am, but I change every day.

Joe L. Hensley has written for many science
fiction and mystery magazines and is the author
of nine novels for the Crime Club, including
Outcasts, Minor Murders, and *A Killing in Gold.*
He often draws upon his extensive legal experience, which includes a term as prosecuting attorney for the Fifth Judicial Circuit of the State
of Indiana. He is now a judge of the Circuit
Court and lives in Madison, Indiana. FINAL
DOORS is his first collection of short stories.